When Does Life Begin?

Brandi Easterling Collins

LUMINESCE
•PUBLISHING•

Luminesce Publishing books may be ordered through booksellers or by contacting:

Luminesce Publishing
www.luminescepublishing.com

LUMINESCE
•PUBLISHING•

Illustrations and cover photo: Designed by Freepik
Cover and interior design © Luminesce Publishing
Author photos © Felisha Weaver Photography

ISBN: 979-8-9854169-0-9 (paperback)
ISBN: 979-8-9854169-1-6 (ebook)
Library of Congress Control Number: 2023915907

This novel is dedicated to my mother,
Opal, who has always been supportive,
and to my uncle, Howard Easterling, Jr., who told me
when I was a kid to never give up my dreams of being a writer.

Acknowledgements:

Thank you to my husband, Jonathan, for being generally awesome, supporting my dreams, and offering opinions from a male perspective. Thank you to my children, Drew and Meredith, for allowing me time to write and read.

Thank you to my wonderful friends and beta readers, Alisha, Devin, Melissa, and Sarah for their valuable feedback and support of this story.

Thank you for the continued support of my readers.

Thank you to my favorite mutts, Peanut and Roscoe, for being a captive audience during my late-night read-aloud editing sessions.

Chapter 1
May 29, 2024

I've wanted to be an actress for as long as I can remember because it goes well with lying, one of my exceptional skills. Just don't tell my mother; she raised me with this whole moral code I knew I'd break the moment I met Jason five years ago.

It was my second day of college classes, and I was a scared, shy, and awkward girl who'd only been kissed as part of a play. The only time I felt like myself was when I was pretending to be someone else on stage. But that was freshman year, and sometimes it seems like a lifetime has passed since then.

Now, I'm sitting on a bench at the cemetery. Marienne's grave is in front of me, and I wish she were here instead. It's hard to believe she's been gone a year. She'd died the day before my birthday, so now I'm getting ready to pass another one without her.

I'd met her freshman year at our university, and it felt like we'd known each other forever from day one. She was the brightest, most attractive person in the room the day I chose a bean bag next to her in our theatre class.

A bottle-blonde since her early teens, Marienne had shined in a crowd—channeling Marilyn Monroe both on and off the stage. We were fast friends and soon roommates for the next four years once we'd sorted out everything with the housing office.

Marienne was brutally honest. She never liked Jason as boyfriend material since she'd known him her whole life. Despite that, she'd go to bat for me with him anytime she had the chance. Though she didn't understand my endless faith in him, she trusted my instincts and figured he must have had some redeeming qualities only I could see. She wasn't quiet in her opinion that I deserved better than her "man-child" first cousin (her words, not mine). Maybe I did, but it's hard to hear criticism when you're in love, and even harder to comprehend when you feel a soulmate-like allurement to a person—a connection you can't even explain to yourself.

"Marienne, I miss you so much." The wind blew through the cemetery and shook the fresh bouquet of daffodils I'd placed on her grave.

If she were here, Marienne would say, "*Of course, my dear, because I'm the most fabulous person you've ever known or ever will know.*"

Modesty wasn't part of her unique grace. Acting came naturally to her, and she could turn on the waterworks in an instant for a scene. I learned so much from her during our brief friendship. For me and those who loved her, she is forever twenty-one, her image permanently etched in our minds.

Out of the corner of my eye, I catch movement on the gravel walkway beside me that draws me away from my thoughts. As I turn to face the other cemetery visitor, my breath catches in my throat. I haven't seen him since before Marienne died, but I'd know him anywhere. Jason Caldwell—the man who'd shattered my heart.

He stands still for a moment before taking a seat beside me like no time has passed and then speaks, unsure of the power of his own voice. "Hey, Lydia. How you been?"

The nerve of him.

Chapter 2
Five Years Earlier
August 20, 2019

If my first day of college had taught me anything, it was that I was capable of making new friends. In my theatre class, I'd already formed a connection with an awesome girl—Marienne Caldwell—or she had made friends with me, something like that.

We'd met for lunch and dinner in the cafeteria the first day and already had plans to switch rooms to get away from our terrible roommates in the dorm. Hers was a horrible snorer, and mine spent a lot of time in her car to skirt the campus smoking policy, bringing the odor with her into our room.

My Tuesdays and Thursdays were filled with boring but necessary classes to satisfy my general education requirements. After sitting through early morning Intro to Biology that seemed to drone on forever, I headed into College Algebra and sat near a girl who looked as shy as I still felt even after a successful first day. The curly-haired redhead wrote furiously in her boy band-adorned notebook as our instructor tried to sell us on the joys of College Algebra (spoiler alert: it was not joyous at all).

After class, when all four feet, eleven inches of Vicki stood up, I took my chance at making another friend. "How'd you keep your hand from cramping up with all that writing?" I asked her.

She chuckled at my question. "I don't wanna take this class again," she said. "I hate math and barely passed it in high school. How 'bout you?"

"Math's a necessary evil. I don't love it or hate it. It's just meh, you know? I'm Lydia Dawson."

"Vicki Price," she said, shoving her books into a weathered leather backpack that was already stuffed. When she hoisted it over her shoulders, I worried she'd fall over and get trapped like an overturned turtle. "Do you live in Smith Hall? You look familiar."

"Yeah. First floor."

"Me too. Third floor. I think I saw you move-in day. Did you go to the welcome dance in the quad?"

"Those aren't really my scene," I said, motioning for her to go ahead of me. "But I can fake it if I have to. I stayed in and read a book, but I plan to get involved in some other things. I'm on my way to an Art Club meeting now, and I'll be in the theatre productions since that's my major."

"I suck at art," she said. "Unless it's art history. I want to teach history in a high school."

"That's awesome," I said. "I loved my high school history teacher."

"Would you wanna eat lunch with me later so we could chat some more? Noon? I don't know anyone here yet."

"Sure," I answered with a smile. "Back right corner of the caf? I'll be there with my new friend Marienne."

"Great," she said with a wave as she walked in the opposite direction. "See you there."

And just like that, I'd started another friendship. Since I'd gone to college with only three people from my small high school and hadn't seen any of them so far, I felt pretty good about how things were starting out. My best friend from home, Phoebe Wilson, had planned to go to college with me and had changed her mind before registration, wanting to stick closer to home. I understood she needed to do what felt right for her, but part of me had been worried about losing touch with her.

I made it across campus to the Art Building in less than five minutes. The weather was lovely and sunny, and I realized quickly I'd chosen the wrong shoes. The wedge sandals I'd worn in high school were rubbing blisters on my heels from all the walking and I vowed to toss them into the dumpster as soon as I got back to the dorm later.

After a painful walk up the stairs to the third floor of the Art Building, I collapsed into a chair in the empty classroom to prepare for the meeting. I'd arrived five minutes before the eleven o'clock start time, and after fifteen minutes of waiting, I stood to leave, figuring the meeting had been cancelled or moved to another location.

As I turned toward the door, I saw him. A stocky guy with brown hair braided in pigtails down his chest. He had the clearest pale blue eyes I'd ever seen and a small scruff of hair around his mouth attempting to be a goatee. I stood there like a doofus, unable to speak for a moment. He wasn't the most attractive guy in the world by any means, but there was a radiance about him, and it seemed like we already knew each other...or I was supposed to know him.

"You're not leaving, are you?" he asked. "We're always a little late getting the meeting started. I'm Jason." He stuck out his hand for me to shake. It was covered in black paint, so I stepped back. He looked at his hand and then wiped it on his jeans, which were dragging the ground over his flip-flops. "Oh, sorry. Ink. Occupational hazard. And you are?"

I cleared my throat, still caught in his mesmerizing eyes. "Lydia. Lydia Dawson."

"Hi, Lydia-Lydia Dawson. You an Art major?"

"Just Lydia is fine. I'm not an Art major, but I took art in high school. I'm taking Intro to Drawing. Do I have to be an Art major to join?"

We were interrupted by a girl with a blue mohawk who walked in between us. "No," she said, pushing Jason backward.

"New girl, you can join the club no matter what your major is...now what is it?"

"Theatre."

"Jason...stop scaring away potential new members, especially when they have artistic majors and cool overalls."

I looked down at my overalls, having forgotten what I was wearing or even who I was in Jason's presence. I'd sewn on a few embroidered patches to spruce up the plain denim. Just the mention of my clothing by the mohawk girl—whose clothing was held together by at least a hundred safety pins—made me feel blaringly high school just like my dark brown chin-length haircut and minimal makeup. I looked all of twelve years old and felt it too.

Soon, about ten other people joined us, some wildly dressed and some in standard clothing, and the meeting began. It was the most disorganized production in the history of time during which Jason was elected president, the mohawk girl vice-president (her name was Nora), and me secretary. By the time the meeting was over, we had plans to meet again the following week, and that was about it. At least it would count as getting involved in college when I spoke with my parents later in the week, right?

As I gathered my things after the meeting, I realized I wasn't the last person remaining. Jason was standing in the doorway watching me. I immediately felt self-conscious.

"I've got a cousin who's an actor," he said. "I've never been into acting, but watching plays is pretty fun. I like the fighting scenes with swords or the dramatic choreographed rumbles like you see in those old musicals my mom forced me to watch when I was a kid, like *West Side Story*, which is a retelling of *Romeo and Juliet*."

"I'm familiar with both," I said, not minding him mansplaining my passion in life. Well, not much anyway. He wore his confidence well while I was still practicing exerting my own. "I played Juliet in our play in high school when I was fifteen and was the only sophomore who had a speaking part."

"Of course, you did," Jason said. "You're the perfect blend of innocence and youthful beauty for a role like that." Then he turned and walked away, leaving me unsure if I should take it as a compliment or an insult coming from a guy like him.

The rest of my afternoon was nice. Marienne and Vicki met during lunch, and I could already tell the three of us would get along well and have some adventures. I breathed easier and felt my anxiety about making friends slip away later in the week as the three of us walked to the next welcome week activity of a campus-wide Bingo game.

As Marienne and Vicki walked ahead of me to swipe their student IDs and collect their Bingo cards, I was nearly knocked over by someone stumbling into my side. The shock lessened as I looked up into Jason's eyes.

"Fancy bumping into you here, Lydia," he said.

"H—Hi, Jason, nice to see you."

Marienne turned around and stuck out her tongue at him. "Hey, dork. Shouldn't you have graduated last year?"

"I'm a super senior, dork," he said. "And I was talking to Lydia, not you."

Marienne put her hand on her hip and turned to me. "I see you met my cousin," she said.

Everything seemed to fall into place. I had the fast-track for info on this mysterious guy.

"We're in Art Club together," Jason said, putting his arm around my shoulders as he introduced himself to Vicki.

Electricity raced throughout my body, jump-starting my heart so much I could hear it pounding in my ears.

Jason removed his arm to grab his game card and followed us to a table. I figured a guy like him wouldn't want to hang out with me, but he sat right beside me and goofed off during the game. After I declined his offer of gum, he folded up the wrapper and played with it. Later he threw it at me, exaggerating his innocence when I turned to him with a smirk.

Though I didn't have much experience, I was pretty sure he was flirting with me. I grabbed the gum wrapper and slipped it into my pocket with plans to save it between the pages of my diary. I had a habit of saving little things significant to me. Something told me he would be important.

After lunch on Friday, Vicki and I walked back to our dorm together while Marienne went to her last class. We passed the student health organization passing out condoms and pamphlets about preventing pregnancy and STIs. Vicki turned pink and started walking as fast as her short legs could take her until we were out of earshot of the group.

"I don't know why it bothers me so much," she muttered. "It's not like my boyfriend and I are completely ignorant about S-E-X."

I smiled, amused that Vicki chose to spell out what embarrassed her. "I didn't know you had a boyfriend. How long have you two been together?"

She grinned. "Since the eighth-grade dance, officially, so five years now," she said. "But I've been in school with him since kindergarten. We were friends the whole time, so we kinda grew up together. He's working his family's farm, so I plan to drive home to see him most weekends until I graduate. I think we'll eventually get married, but we're not in a hurry right now, and we're both committed to saving ourselves until then."

"That's sweet."

"Surely I'm not the only virgin on campus."

"Trust me, you're not."

She stopped walking and looked at me. "You too?"

"Yep. It just hasn't happened. I was always too busy to date in high school, so it's never come up." Honestly, I would have made time if anyone I'd liked had asked me out, but my closest guy friends were taken or in the case of my prom date, gay.

"Well, as much as Marienne's cousin was flirting with you last night, it might come up soon if you want it to."

"Who knows?" I had high hopes Jason would be significant in my life. In hindsight, I should've run like hell.

Chapter 3
May 29, 2024

I stare at Jason for the longest time, or maybe I glare at him. It's long enough for my eyes to water from lack of blinking. I brush away the wetness and turn away. The last thing I want is to let him see me cry. He's already seen and caused enough of it for a lifetime.

"I knew you'd be okay," he says after a few seconds have passed.

"There's a lot you don't know," I say. "How the hell do you think I've been? You just left me—again—dropped off the face of the earth. Sure, I'm okay now, but it took a long time. And even so, there are still some bad days."

"I'm sorry."

I have to laugh at the all-too-late apology. "Well, I guess it makes it all okay then. What are you doing here?"

He gestures toward Marienne's headstone. "Same as you, I guess."

I sigh. "I don't even know what to say to you."

"That's a first—you lacking words."

"I'm not sure you deserve my words."

"I'm ready to listen when you're ready to talk."

"Why now? After all this time?"

"I don't know. I guess it's just time."

Though I'd rehearsed many times what I'd say to Jason if I ever saw him again, none of those words come to mind with him in front of me. All I can do is stare blankly into his eyes. He stands up to walk away.

"Wait," I say. "Should I call you when I'm ready to talk?"

He stops walking without turning around. "I lost my phone a while back," he says. "I'll be here next week at the same time. Come find me if you want to talk."

After I watch him walk away. I turn back toward Marienne's grave. My entire midsection throbs with heartache and nausea as I let myself cry without caring who might see or hear me. In the year since Marienne's death, I thought I was finally healing from the loss of Jason too. Though, after seeing him again, I know I've only been lying to myself. Does anyone ever really get over their first love if the relationship fizzles?

Since I'd last seen Jason, I could barely remember the process of mourning our relationship since it coincided with my grief for Marienne. Phoebe and Vicki had been there for me during the last year, as well as my parents and my stepbrother, Luke. And school will be there too, when or if I decide I'm ready to go back. I'm still on the fence about going for my master's, but I know I don't want to live with my parents for much longer. Being there is its own special hell after living on my own for so long.

Now, don't get me wrong, my mom and stepdad, Larry, are wonderful, but staying with them again after being out on my own makes me feel more anxious and unsettled. Luke is away at medical school, and most of my friends from high school have moved on. Luckily, Phoebe still lives nearby after graduating college, and Vicki and I have met halfway to see each other a couple of times since graduation.

My sales associate job at a local department store has kept me sane since the summer after I graduated college last year. It's the distraction of the job I need more than the money. I inherited money from my grandmother, but I'd rather leave it in a savings account to earn interest for now.

Some of the younger workers are fun to hang out with at the movies or the bowling alley when we get off work. I try to keep everything superficial with my coworkers. While I learn more about their lives, I keep my pain private and stick to customer stories and pop culture. They all assume I was burned out after school and wanted a break before grad school. It's easier that way.

When I'm off work and not hanging out with friends or my family, I'm watching movies or shows, reading books, and watching videos of plays on YouTube. I do anything I can to keep my mind occupied. I can't go to bed until I am almost falling over so I can settle down for a dreamless slumber without having to cry myself to sleep.

I learned pretty quickly that going to bed too early could result in vicious nightmares threatening to loosen my grip on reality—and it was already hanging on with threads thin as spiderwebs. The webs got stronger as my meds did—the antidepressants gradually clearing the fog of desperation in my mind.

Even a year later, I don't think I can stop taking the medicine any time soon. Every time I take my pill, I remember Marienne was on her way to pick me up when she died. I can't even remember where we'd planned to go that night; I only remember I was sad because Jason hadn't contacted me after an ultimatum I'd given him right before my graduation. Another hour, and I might have been in the car with her.

Chapter 4
August 27, 2019

After a weekend full of involvement activities, Marienne had settled in as my new roommate, and I was getting the hang of going to classes without having to pull out my schedule to confirm. Vicki was a frequent visitor in our room, and the three of us ate almost all our meals together. I only had one class with each of my new friends, but I didn't feel out of place among the other freshmen getting used to a different tempo like I was. I knew things would change each year as I was able to take more classes related to my major, and then I'd see the same people all the time.

I spoke to my mom and grandma on the phone a couple of times to report how much I was enjoying college. And I was, no lies needed. I'd worried I might be homesick, but with friends and plenty of things to do, I wasn't feeling it so far. Of course, I knew it might change, but I tried not to worry about it too much. I already planned to only go home to visit about once a month because I didn't want to be a college kid who was home every weekend. I needed to experience being on my own to grow up.

Seeing Jason again at the Art Club meeting was good. I found myself studying his profile as I took notes about his announcements for the group. My heart sputtered a bit, and my hands got all clammy just being near him despite reminding myself I was too old for a junior high kind of crush, and he probably thought I was too young for him anyway. Marienne had told me Jason would be twenty-three in February and I'd just turned eighteen in May. Maybe I was too young.

Apparently, he'd already volunteered the club to paint faces at the upcoming campus carnival, host a booth for community Halloween, participate in the nonperishable food sculpture contest at Thanksgiving, and paint windows at the bookstore to celebrate the holiday season.

In addition to our weekly meetings and loose plans for some cultural field trips, it was a lot, but I figured that's what involvement in college was like. Surely, I'd find some time to study and practice lines for theatre productions.

I was still taking notes to record everything after Jason had dismissed the meeting and everyone else had left the classroom. Then someone blocked out the sunlight from the window in front of me and cast a shadow across my notebook. I looked up to find Jason standing in front of me.

"You don't have to write down every word I said," he teased. "It's okay if you just want to record the meeting with your phone and use one of those text-to-speech programs. I guess I should've mentioned it earlier. It's what I did when I was secretary my second year in the club."

"I didn't think of it," I told him. "But if you want me to do that, I will next time. I'm sorry."

He sat down beside me and nudged my shoulder. "It's fine if you'd prefer to do it your way, but it looks like you might get carpal tunnel problems if you keep writing at that speed. You should save your hands for activities that are more fun."

I felt like a fool as my cheeks flamed. "And what might those activities be?" Wrong. I wasn't a fool before, at least not until I opened my mouth.

"Oh, you know, drawing, painting, holding tacos...the possibilities are endless."

"Well, I hope to get better at drawing and painting to help with set backgrounds. I'm not sure I'll get many parts as a freshman, but I still want to be involved as much as I can."

"I know a lot of the upperclassmen in the program, I could put in a good word for you."

"You've never seen me act. Maybe you should put in a good word for Marienne. I bet you've seen her."

He laughs. "I went to all her plays in junior high and high school, the community theatres during the summers. She'll demand attention all on her own."

"How do you know I won't do that too—all on my own?" It seemed like a good time to practice boldness, not a natural personality trait for me off-stage.

Jason moved forward in his chair to get closer to me and then leaned back like he was studying me. "Because you're incredibly shy, and I don't see you speaking up for yourself very easily. You probably push through the stage fright and do an incredible job, but I can see you're nervous right now."

"Am not. I'm fine." Lies. All lies. I thought I might pass out.

"You have tells. They're easy to see this close, but I can understand how no one would notice from the audience." Jason chuckled as he stood up to leave. "You have sweat beading around your hairline, and your pulse is popping in your neck. So, either you've got a lot of nerves about your upcoming theatre class, or you find me incredibly sexy, and it makes you nervous."

I immediately covered my neck with my hand and watched him walk out the door without turning back. Did I really have tells? I guess I did since he could see I was nervous around him. Too old for me or not, he was interested and so was I. I hadn't imagined our interaction. I wasn't sure what to do except wait and see what might happen next. I definitely wasn't bold enough to make the first move.

Chapter 5
May 30, 2024

I remember as a teenager—around fifteen or so—thinking I'd have everything figured out by the time I turned twenty-three. Back then, it seemed like such a magical age. Well, I'm here to report I was misguided. I still don't know anything. Happy birthday to me.

Last year's celebration never happened, and I hadn't wanted it to since I'd learned of Marienne's death early in the morning on my twenty-second birthday. Of course, my mother had always told me at some point, birthdays just became like regular days for some people. I didn't have the privilege of forgetting mine enough for it to be an ordinary day now, and probably wouldn't in the future either.

Mom insisted we celebrate this year, so I've agreed to a small dinner with her, my stepfather, and my stepbrother. Plus, I've invited Phoebe and her boyfriend Sam. I don't have to work today, so at least I have until seven this evening to collect myself.

I hardly slept at all last night. Talking to Jason at the cemetery yesterday left me rattled and drowning in memories I've tried to avoid for the past year. I can't remember fun times with Marienne without thinking of Jason, and I can't reminisce about the good times with him without acknowledging how much I miss them both. I'm glad I still have Phoebe, and I have memories with Vicki that are separate from Marienne. I couldn't bear to lose them too.

During our last appointment, my therapist pushed me toward some things I'm just not ready for yet. I assume her assistant will reach out soon since I'd left in a hurry and failed to schedule my next appointment.

Healing is hard work and takes as much time as it takes, according to Dr. Benson, but I worry she's become frustrated with my progress. I tell her the truth for the most part, even though I haven't stopped lying to my family—by omission mainly. I can't tell them about my trip to the cemetery because they'll worry it isn't healthy for me. I don't know how to make them understand it's something I need to do right now.

Maybe I was foolish to fall so deeply in love with the first guy I ever dated, but I can't go back and change the past. I just have to keep living with the consequences and feelings still locked deep within my heart. Despite how much heartache Jason caused me during our times together and apart, I think I've cried more this past year than I have any other time in my life.

If I could, I'd want to go back in time, but I'm not sure where I'd start. Would I be able to save my father? Could I stop Marienne's accident? Or go back and turn Jason down when he'd asked me out to avoid future heartache? I'd give anything to not have to feel the constant absence of something or someone.

I know I should "get back out there" at some point so I won't end up spending my life alone, but getting over Jason has been hard. It's been more than a year since I've been kissed or held, and I miss the closeness of it. But sometimes I wonder if I miss Jason or if I miss who I was before him or how I felt when things were going well between us. I don't know if I'll ever figure it out.

I spend the day being lazy, streaming some old musicals on my laptop. I put off showering and getting dressed until late afternoon, treating the day like a sick day, although I'm not sick. I'm just tired—tired of having to pretend everything's getting better when I know I have more work to do. How I'm reacting to having seen Jason again is proof of that. And I can't keep my mind off him long enough to focus on anything productive.

Larry is home from work by six, and Luke arrives soon afterward. My mom parks in the garage only moments before Phoebe and Sam pull up behind her in the driveway right at seven. Luke and Larry help Mom unload the pizza and ice cream cake so we can get the party started. I ignore the balloons adorning the cake and tell myself this is just a regular celebration on a day that doesn't remind me of loss.

Sam looks more grown up than he did when we graduated high school. His baby face has filled out and he could easily pass for thirty with his neatly trimmed beard, and I want to address him as Mr. Mitchell instead of his first name. Sam rests his hand on the back of Phoebe's chair while she tells us about her plans for summer classes, and then he talks about his latest welding jobs. Phoebe watches him with such pride, and I miss being in love.

Luke talks about his upcoming move to Tennessee to start work at St. Jude Children's Hospital, and I realize how quickly the two weeks until he leaves will pass. And then it's my turn in the hot seat. I tell everyone how excited I am to start a summerlong acting workshop next week since I've been away from the theatre since I graduated college last year.

Everyone wants more details, but I don't have anything else to share — the whole program is shrouded in secrecy. It ends with an audition which could lead to a big part in a new play that will tour all over the United States. It's the best chance I have right now to get my name out there if I ever want to be a big name on the stage someday.

When the celebration is over and we've all had our cake, I walk Phoebe and Sam outside. She lingers while Sam goes to start the car.

"Are you doing okay?" she asks. "I know it's a hard day for you."

"I'm hanging in there. I had to go to Russellville yesterday, so I went and put flowers on Marienne's grave since I was nearby. It was hard, but I'm feeling okay about it."

Phoebe smiles and hugs me tightly. "I love you, Lyds."

After my friends have gone home, I go out to our deck and lie back in a lounge chair to look at the stars. Luckily, it's a clear night. I can't remember the last time I came out here so late or even took the time to enjoy the sky. When the deck door slides open and closes, I don't even turn to look because I know Luke's footsteps, strong and steady, even in his flip-flops.

"You're just asking for mosquito bites," he tells me as he stretches out in the other chair.

"Worth it."

"Twenty-three. I still feel like you should be a little kid."

"Me too, sometimes, but here I am. Still living with my parents."

"Not for long," Luke says, standing up again. He walks over to the patio table and lights a large citronella candle sitting in the middle of it. I can't stand the scent, but it does help keep the pesky bugs away.

"At least for the summer until I know about the play."

Luke returns to his chair. "It's okay. You've had a rough year, and there's no shame in taking some time to take care of yourself. You are doing that, right? Your meds, therapy?"

"Yes, Dr. Carmichael," I say, smiling. His checking on me doesn't feel as humiliating as when my mom does it. "The meds are helping, and I plan to see Dr. Benson again soon. Things got busy, so I missed this month."

"Meaning you had to cancel an appointment, or you never made one?"

Damn it. It's been more difficult to lie to Luke since he saved my life last June. It's like he developed a Lydia-themed lie detector. "The second one. But I promise I'll call and schedule something for next week. I just needed a break."

"She upset you?"

"It's just hard. It's been a year since the accident, and I miss Marienne, and even though I shouldn't, I miss Jason. More than anything, I miss feeling like myself. I don't think any number of pills is going to change that." I can barely make out Luke's face in the ambient light outside, but I feel him looking at me, raising an eyebrow, his signature expression. "I'm sorry. Poor choice of words."

"Just promise me you won't quit therapy. I don't think you're ready. You seem sad and distant today, and I get it. Your birthday will always be a reminder, but I don't want you to let the sadness consume you again."

"I won't let it, Luke," I say as I get up and move to his chair to hug him. "And I'm so sorry for...well, for everything you had to do."

He squeezes me tightly before letting go to look me in the eyes. "Lydia, you're my sister, and getting help for you wasn't an inconvenience. It's what any brother would do, and nobody wants to lose someone they love—especially like that."

"Thank you."

"You don't have to keep thanking me."

"But I do. You saved my life, and I'm grateful."

Luke nods and puts his arm around my shoulder. I couldn't have dreamt up a better brother, and I hope he knows how much I love him.

Chapter 6
August 31, 2019

Staying in the dorms over Labor Day weekend was one part trying to prove my independence and another part my mom and stepdad worrying about me driving home when there might be drunk drivers on the road. I hated to remind them it was always a possibility.

Almost everyone else had gone home, including Marienne and Vicki. Campus was a ghost town. The dorms were deserted, and so was the cafeteria except for a small group of international students whose homes were too far away for a weekend visit. When an unfamiliar number popped up on my phone as I was walking back to my room after eating brunch, I answered the call when I normally would have let it go to voicemail.

Jason calling me wasn't expected at all, even though I'd shared my number on the Art Club roster. And I certainly hadn't expected him to ask me out on a date for that evening. I felt like a loser for not already having plans on a Saturday night, but then I realized neither did he or he wouldn't be asking. I had a whole conversation in my head in the ten seconds it took me to agree to go out with him after he'd asked.

After ending the call, my whole body was shaking. I'd never had a real date. All through high school I'd gone to dances with groups of friends, and my senior prom date had been the only gay guy in our class. Sure, I'd had crushes on several guys, but nothing had ever worked out. Elementary boyfriends didn't count when it came to real dating experience.

Hell, my first kiss at fifteen had been part of our *Romeo and Juliet* school play, and I didn't consider it as counting either. At college, I'd hoped to break free from my lack of real-life romance skills.

I changed clothes at least twenty times before I settled on the first outfit I'd tried. Basic distressed jeans, a black V-neck t-shirt, and black flat sandals. I put on minimal makeup, some basic gold hoop earrings, and my favorite necklace bearing a pendant of the masks of comedy and tragedy. I combed out my chin-length hair and scrunched it in my hands as I dried it to try to give it some natural body, but it hung flat and straight as always. I glanced in the mirror before grabbing my small clutch which was just big enough for my phone, ID cards, and some lip gloss. I looked as pretty as I could without looking like I'd tried too hard.

Five minutes after eight o'clock, Jason arrived outside my dorm. He smiled at me as I pushed through the double doors to meet him. He was wearing old jeans and a plain grey t-shirt. His hair was parted down the middle and hung loosely down his back, and he had two-day-old stubble on his cheeks. Perfectly casual as I'd expected. I breathed a sigh of relief I wasn't over- or under-dressed.

"You ready?" he asked, leading the way to his small blue truck.

I followed him and climbed into the truck after he'd opened the door. I took a couple of calming breaths as I fastened my seatbelt. He walked around the front to get in and then fastened his belt before starting the engine. The stereo blared as soon as the engine rumbled to life, and he quickly turned down the volume.

"Sorry about that," he said. "Since you're new here, I want to take you to the best burger place in town. I hope that's okay."

"Sounds great."

"A friend from my printmaking class is going to meet us there with his girlfriend. I haven't hung out with him for a while, and I figured we'd all get along."

"I'm looking forward to meeting some of your friends."

"Did Mari fill your head with all kinds of embarrassing stories about me?"

I laughed. "She and I haven't talked about you at all."

It wasn't a lie...exactly. Marienne and I had texted back and forth earlier in the day while she was on break from her part-time job at a farm supply store. She'd warned me to be careful, and I'd assured her I would. Jason had recently gotten out of a relationship and was trying to be "just friends" with his last girlfriend. It didn't seem too alarming.

"Should I be worried?" I asked as we pulled into the burger place's parking lot. The sign read: A Hole in the Wall Burgers.

He looked at me with a smirk. "Probably."

I got out of the truck before Jason had a chance to walk around and get me.

I was surprised to see Jason's friends were in their late twenties or early thirties, much older than him. Davis and Wren were nice enough, and they seemed genuinely interested in what I had to say. Both were big into musicals and theatre—and art in general, so the conversation never dulled as we ate our burgers, which were incredible. I still felt like a child out of place at the adult table.

"It was great to meet you, Lydia," Davis said as he and Wren got ready to leave. "It's been so long since we've been able to go out with other people and have an actual intelligent conversation."

"It was good to meet you both too," I said.

"We'll have to do this again soon," Wren said.

I looked at Jason, who didn't say anything as he headed to the trash can to return our tray. Davis followed him.

"That would be nice," I told Wren.

"How long have you and Jason been dating?" she asked.

I laughed. "That's a loaded question. This is our first date."

Wren raised her eyebrows. "Oh."

I wasn't able to say anything else because the guys came back. Jason and I waved our goodbyes as Davis and Wren pulled away in his old VW Bug.

Jason nudged my shoulder. "So, are you ready to go back to your dorm?"

"Not really," I said. "I enjoyed meeting your friends, but I was hoping to get to know you better."

"Good," he said, leading the way to his truck. "I know somewhere we can go."

By the time Jason and I arrived at the old lookout point, the sun had already set. We were the only two people in the dirt and gravel parking lot. There was a rock wall overlooking a cliff full of trees from what I could see before he shut off his headlights.

"Not many people come here anymore since the highway bypass opened," he told me as I joined him to sit on the rock wall. "It's quiet here, and legend has it if you're real quiet, you can hear train whistles on the abandoned track below."

"Hmm, I've never heard of this place before."

"I grew up about ten miles down the road. My parents have a few acres outside of town."

"So, you didn't go far from home for college then. My parents are almost two hours away."

"Well, technically, I still live with my parents. There's an in-law suite my grandma lived in for a while before she died. I moved in there when I started college so it's kinda like my own apartment."

"It has to be better than living in the dorms. I don't think my original roommate knew how to shower. I'm glad Marienne and I were able to switch rooms."

Jason scrunched up his face. "Showering's very important," he said with a laugh. "You smell like you know how to shower."

I could feel my cheeks brightening as I turned away to check out the view. "One of my many talents."

"So, why theatre?"

"I don't know. I guess it's the only thing that made sense to me since I want to be an actress. Why art?"

"It's the only thing I've ever been good at."

"Same here. It's what I've always wanted to do. On stage, I'm not me...I'm anyone...someone spectacular...someone not so shy or awkward. It's like I come alive when I'm pretending to be someone else."

"You seem pretty alive to me." He brushed my cheek, sending tingles down my neck and into my stomach. "Warm to the touch and everything."

"Good to know."

"Listen." He pointed toward the ravine.

A light rumble started in the distance and seemed to be coming from below. I listened intently to see if I could hear the train whistle. Jason had moved closer, and I could feel his thigh touching mine. No train whistle, but I could feel air on my cheek as Jason exhaled.

When I turned to my left, he was looking at me. I felt drawn to him, and the next thing I knew, he was kissing me...or I was kissing him...we were kissing. It wasn't part of a play, and no one yelled "cut" as if we were in a rehearsal. My heart was pounding, and I felt lightheaded. I had no idea what to do, so I pulled away to avoid passing out.

Jason kept his arm around me. "Did you hear the train whistle?" he asked.

I leaned against his shoulder. "I couldn't hear anything."

"That's too bad."

"No one's ever kissed me before," I blurted. "I mean, not because they wanted to. For plays and acting exercises." I wanted to disappear into the ravine to hide from my embarrassment.

"You've been missing out, then," he said. "What was it in *Gone With the Wind*, that Rhett told Scarlett? Something about needing to be kissed often by someone who knows how to do it?"

"Something like that," I said. "I'm surprised you've seen it."

"Mom made me watch all sorts of old movies when I was a kid, in addition to all the musicals she loved."

A car pulled up behind us, and Jason dropped his arm off my shoulders.

Three high-school-aged boys bailed out of the car. "Aw, man," one said. "Did we miss the train whistles?"

Jason helped me off the rock wall. "Nah, man," he said. "I think you got here just in time. We haven't heard anything." He led me back to his truck.

"Wanna go somewhere else?" Jason asked as he started the engine.

"Yes." My head was still spinning from our interrupted moment, and I really needed to pee. The only thing I knew with certainty was I didn't want our evening to end.

A few minutes later, Jason pulled into the parking lot of a deserted city park. He led me to a darkened pavilion near some public restrooms. I excused myself for a moment, thankful for anything. The toilets weren't too nasty from what I could see with my phone's flashlight, so I was able to find relief and head back outside. Jason was no longer sitting where I'd left him at the picnic table. His truck was still dark, so I figured he'd ducked into the men's room.

Suddenly, a man grabbed my shoulders from behind and I elbowed him in the stomach before he could grab my arms.

"Whoa, there, killer," Jason said, turning me around.

I punched him in the shoulder, a move I would normally only pull on my stepbrother. "You scared me half to death, jerk!"

"Ow," he said, rubbing his shoulder. "Remind me not to piss you off."

"You shouldn't need reminding."

He grinned at me like he knew he was too charming for me to stay mad at him. It was true; he was. I moved closer to him again, and he pulled me into his arms. "So...can I kiss you again?"

I nodded and let him kiss me. Soon, he pulled me over to the top of the picnic table where we stretched out together, surrounded by fireflies as we listened to the crickets and cicadas in the distance. We talked about everything and nothing at all well into the early morning.

Before dawn, Jason grinned and turned to me again, and we made out right there on the table, our own private spot in the middle of the city where it felt like we were the only two people in the world.

Chapter 7
June 3, 2024

My upcoming audition is not exactly Broadway, but it's a start with a large theatre group that would put me touring several cities, including Chicago, Denver, Houston, and Seattle to name a few. For the next ten weeks, I'm taking a workshop with other actors and actresses, and then we'll all have to be ready to audition for the producers. One of my favorite professors from college nominated me for the workshop and even found a grant to help cover the tuition.

All the actors are going in blind. No one has read the play or seen it performed because it's brand new. All I know is the description of the female lead seems like it was written for me. Young woman in her early twenties, unlucky in love, no stranger to heartache. I could've written the story.

As a precaution, I have my temperature checked at the registration table and show my COVID-19 vaccination card.

Walking into the theatre is a bit nerve-wracking, but I know I'm among like-minded souls as soon as I walk in the door. There are several women huddled near the stage who look up at me. I force myself to smile at them, and all but one return it quickly. The last woman studies me, looking me up and down for a few seconds before squinting and turning away. There's a diva in every group, and I think I've found her in this one.

A few guys are milling around in different places. Some are staring at their phones, and a few have scripts in their hands—some last-minute prep for the monologues we're expected to deliver today to gauge our experience and talent before we get started. I've chosen one of Emily's from *Our Town*, which I hope is a safe choice. I didn't want to go too old with Shakespeare, and I didn't want to go too new with a contemporary choice.

"Ah, good choice on the monologue," a male voice says from beside me. I glance over to a tall, light-haired guy with a nice smile and warm brown eyes. "I love that play."

I clutch the book to my chest. "It's one of my favorites."

He sticks out his hand. "I'm Kolton—with a 'K' because my parents wanted me to match my twin sister, Kendra."

"Lydia." I take his hand. "Nice to meet you."

A whistle pierces the air, startling us both.

A tall woman with chopsticks sticking out of her messy bun drops her whistle. "Choose a partner of the opposite sex and be ready for introductions in fifteen minutes."

Kolton lets go of my hand. "Wanna partner up? Unless you'd prefer someone else."

"No...yes...I mean, yes, I'll partner with you, and I don't know anyone else here. Do you know anyone?"

He looks around the room. "I don't recognize anyone."

"I guess we better get started. I have a feeling she'll make us introduce each other."

"I have the same feeling," Kolton says as we walk to a section of seating near the stage.

I learn the basics about Kolton during our brief conversation. He's two years older than me and works as a carpenter, swearing it worked for Harrison Ford, so he'd see if it worked for him. He'd thought about teaching with his communications degree but realized he didn't like being around children enough to do so. I can relate to him there.

He and his sister left the church he grew up in after the congregation tried to "pray away the gay" several years ago. Makes sense. The first guy I've found even remotely attractive since Jason would end up being outside the realm of possibility—though I didn't get that vibe from him.

While Kolton is open about having taken a break from dating since his ex cheated on him last year, I keep my heart locked up tight. I can already tell we'll be friends, but I'm not ready to share so much. I'm still struggling with my feelings for Jason and unsure how to move on—if that's even possible. Especially after seeing him at the cemetery and knowing I might see him there again. I want to see him almost as much as I dread facing another painful conversation.

The shrill whistle breaks up my thoughts and we begin our introductions.

I learn the tall woman is Bernetta, the acting coach hired for the workshop. She tells us she's been an acting coach for thirty years, which I find amazing considering she doesn't look a day over forty-five. I figure her pale skin hasn't been sun-burned in her whole life despite how close she is to it at her height (six-foot-one, she tells us).

All the actors are between the ages of twenty-one and thirty, and there are only twelve of us in the class, six women and six men. We're split into two groups and told to get used to those people since we'd be rehearsing together. The playwright is a native Arkansan and wanted the younger roles to go to other native Arkansans since she wanted authentic accents. Next, we learn a second class will take place once the primaries are chosen to work with established older actors for some of the other parts in the play.

Everything is locked down, and no one in the workshop will get to see the actual play until they have been awarded a part. Everything we do will be based on acting exercises and well-known scenes from other plays and musicals. Kolton leans toward me and raises his eyebrows, mouthing "WTF."

He's right; I've never been part of anything so secretive before, either. It's exciting and exactly what I need as a distraction from the rest of my life. But it's also more than a distraction; it's what I wish for all the time.

With me in my group are Kolton, Tanya, Tom, Nel, and Jake, and we're all different enough for me to remember their names easily. The other group holds the diva with her fitting name of Divine, two other women, Makenna and Emily, plus guys John, Jensen, and Matt. The brief introductions go off without a hitch, but I can't remember much about my classmates in the other group, but I know I'll learn more about them as the workshop continues.

Once we're all finished speaking about our partners, it's time for our prepared monologues. Luckily, I'm the only one in the group who recites from *Our Town*. Several people perform musical numbers, but not Kolton. He presents a scene from *The Vagina Monologues*, which I find to be a bold choice. He speaks with such grace and not a single moment is tongue-in-cheek. I decide against falling in love with him on the spot because of the whole gay thing—no sense in diving headfirst into unrequited love again. Oh well. I guess I can love him as a friend.

"The last thing I want you to do today is stand where you are and tell the group about a moment of profound grief in your life," Bernetta says. "This play is quite emotional, so every part will need to pull from deep feelings for authenticity. If that's a problem for anyone, you should drop out now and request a refund. I don't want to waste your time or mine. Any issues?"

We all look around and shake our heads. I'm not naïve enough to believe no one else has experienced grief, but I wonder who among us is the most damaged by life so far.

"Lydia," Bernetta continues. "We'll start with you, and everyone please state your full names again so we can make sure we learn everyone's names quickly."

I stand and take a deep breath. "Hi everyone. I'm Lydia Dawson. Unfortunately, I've been accustomed to death since I was a kid after my father died suddenly when I was five years old, followed by his father. I don't think I understood death enough at that point to share the same level of grief with my mom, who'd lost her husband, or my grandmother, who'd lost her only child and later her husband.

"Even when I was in middle school and lost my grandparents on my mom's side, it was just expected the elderly would die from their poor health, and I accepted it despite my sadness. And I was forced to accept the death of my last grandmother from COVID four years ago.

"But the most profound grief I've felt is from losing one of my best friends in a car accident last year. Marienne was young, beautiful, and vibrant. She was an actress too, and I have no doubt she would have been a big name someday. It isn't fair some people have to leave us so young. She was only twenty-one and we'd just graduated from college where we'd met and been roommates for four years. She should have had a whole life to look forward to, but she didn't, and it's not fair." I sit and wipe a stray tear from my eye. Kolton reaches over and squeezes my hand.

"I'm sorry about your friend," Bernetta says, clutching her fist over her heart. "Keep her close. Next, Kolton."

Kolton lets go of my hand and stands from his chair beside me. "I'm Kolton Black, and I'm not sure if I can follow Lydia," he says. "I've been fortunate with no deaths in my family or friend group. My grandparents are still living and in good health for their ages, so I'm grateful. The biggest moment of grief I've had was leaving a church I'd grown up with and loved for many years. I don't regret leaving for a second after what they did to my twin sister once she came out as a lesbian because I couldn't stay at a place that ousted my sister and screamed at her, saying she'd burn in hell for being gay."

Wait. His sister? It meant Kolton wasn't talking about himself and the church earlier. Now he has the potential to be dangerous to my heart.

"I had a bit of a crisis of faith," Kolton continues. "I'm in a better place now, but I know I'll never walk through the doors of that church ever again, and it has nothing to do with my relationship with God. I have to keep it separate or I'll go crazy."

As Kolton sits down, I return his support by offering my hand. He smiles at me, and my heart drops into my stomach. He's a great guy, and I know he'll be important in my life.

Tanya stands next to tell her story. She's a pretty, petite Black woman with dark hair and a shiny gold hoop in her nostril that matches the larger ones in each ear. "Hi, everyone," she says. "My name's Tanya Johnson and the worst grief I've felt was watching my dad get arrested for gang violence in Little Rock when I was ten. He was the only parent I had since my mom left when I was little. He couldn't get out of it and ended up killing a guy in self-defense, but the law didn't see it that way. I went to live with my aunt out of state afterward and got into acting at my new school. My dad died in jail, and now here I am. I'm determined to have a better life than my parents."

Tom takes center stage next, choosing not to stay at his seat like the rest of us. His shoulder-length black hair is slicked back, and he's dressed like the workshop's an audition for John Travolta's part in *Grease*–dark rolled-up jeans, a white t-shirt, and a black leather jacket. "I'm Tom Chang," he says. "My parents are second-generation Chinese Americans and really big on education–falling into all the typical stereotypes of my people. My whole life I've been disappointing them by wanting to act rather than be a doctor or an engineer or some other bullshit that would crush my soul.

"When I was a teenager, right before leaving for college, I had this big fight with my parents. As I was driving away, I accidentally backed over our dog, Scrabbles. I was devastated; I loved my dog. I couldn't tell my family and cause even more disappointment, so I took Scrabbles and buried him in the woods behind my friend's house. My parents and my little sister thought he ran away and even called the shelters and tacked up flyers about our missing dog. It was months before they accepted Scrabbles wasn't coming back." Tom wipes a few tears from his face and sits back in his chair across from me. I give him a half-smile, feeling his pain.

"Thank you for sharing, Tom," Bernetta says. "Jake, you're up."

Jake is a tall and lanky white guy with a buzz cut. He stands and sticks his hands in the back pockets of his ripped jeans. His arms are covered in tattoos, and his t-shirt advertises a heavy metal concert from a band I've never heard of. "I'm Jake Winston, twenty-two years old, a mostly recovered drug addict. I got into acting in juvie and it helped me kick the heavy stuff, though I can't quite give up vaping. When I was fifteen, right before I got into serious trouble, my girlfriend at the time overdosed on Fentanyl and died right in front of me. We'd broken into an abandoned house and started a fire in the fireplace there. Some neighbors called the cops and they happened to pull up right as Lexi was dying. I miss her every day, but getting arrested that night saved my life, and I think Lexi would want me to keep on going."

Wow. Jake's story makes my heart ache for him. He's not crying like Tom, but his jaw is tight and the muscles in his arms are twitching as he rocks back and forth on the balls of his feet.

Next comes Nelanie—not to be confused with Melanie—which is too ordinary, according to her, though she prefers to go by Nel. Her hair is long and jet black, parted down the middle, reminding me of old photos of Cher in the 1970s.

Nel had gotten pregnant while in high school and chose to give the baby up for adoption after her boyfriend dumped her. She'd wanted to keep her daughter, but she knew she'd curse them to a life of poverty since her parents had kicked her out after learning about the pregnancy. Nel had managed to work her way through the rest of high school and community college while staying with her great aunt until the old lady died several weeks ago, leaving Nel the small house. Her dream is to be an actress, and her aunt's dying wish had been for Nel to land a part in this play.

Most of the other grief stories touch my heart too. The second group goes while my mind is still reeling just from the stories my group shared. I avoid rolling my eyes when Divine's moment of grief is getting a scratch on her brand-new Tesla. Next, there are two lost grandparent stories, a lost parent, another lost friend story, and the loss of a special teacher. Bernetta shares she lost her son in a drowning accident when he was only twenty and how the grief broke up her marriage. Then we all join hands in a show of solidarity to validate everyone's pain.

After the workshop ends, Kolton catches up as I'm walking to my car. "Hey, Lydia, wait up!"

I toss my tote bag into the car and turn around. "Hey," I say. "It was intense in there, hearing all the grief stories."

"It was." He kicks a piece of gravel across the parking lot and pulls out his phone. "Would you mind sharing your number? I figure it'd be good for us to have a way to get in touch to talk about the exercises and stuff."

"Sure." I take his phone and enter my number, sending myself a text. I pull my phone out of my back pocket and reply with my name. "There you go."

He grins at me as he takes his phone. I smile back at him. It's been a long time since I've done that, and I can't understand why I feel a little guilty about it.

Chapter 8
September 1, 2019

By the time Jason dropped me off at my dorm, it was almost daybreak on Sunday. I took off my shoes as soon as I got in the lobby so I wouldn't disturb any of the few people who had stayed for the weekend and might be sleeping. Walking barefoot to my room on the first floor felt strange and new. Plus, I hadn't been awake at that time of day for as long as I could remember.

Marienne had gone home for the long weekend, so I was alone when I shut my room door and locked it behind me. As I leaned against the closed door, my skin tingled, and my vision went blurry for a second. Soon, bile rose up in my throat and I barely made it to the sink before I threw up. After a minute or two, I was fine but shaky. I rinsed my mouth with water, popped a couple of chewable antacids, and crashed into my bed fully clothed.

What felt like minutes later, I woke to the sound of my phone vibrating on top of the mini-fridge beside my bed. It was late afternoon, and my grandmother was calling.

"Hi, Grammy," I answered, stifling a yawn.

"Oh, Lydia, I hope I didn't wake you," she replied.

"No ... not at all. I just finished exercising."

"Good girl," she said. Grammy was big on staying healthy. "Your mother said you had a date last night, so I wanted to see how it went. You didn't stay out too late, did you?"

"I got in early."

"Was he a gentleman?"

"He was very nice, Grammy. We had burgers with another couple and went for a nice walk in the park." *Actually, I let him kiss me and stick his hand under my shirt in the park.*

"That sounds lovely, dear." Rustling filled the silence and I had to pull the phone away from my ear. "I'm heading to my bridge game, so I'll let you go. Keep taking care of yourself."

"I will. Love you."

"Love you more."

I let my phone fall to the bed beside me. If memory served me correctly, I'd crashed for ten hours or so. My empty stomach protested with a groan, and honestly, I was relieved to feel hungry. I grabbed a yogurt out of the fridge without even leaving my bed and fished a spoon from the mug on top. It wasn't much of a meal, but I'd slept through brunch time in the cafeteria, so it was my only option if I didn't want to drive somewhere to get food. I was too sleep-drunk to even consider it, and I was in desperate need of a shower and a serious oral hygiene session.

Choosing to brush my teeth immediately after finishing the yogurt and downing a half-bottle of water, I was startled at the sight of my reflection. My hair was a rat's nest and there was mascara smeared all around my eyes. Any trace of the lipstick I'd worn the evening before was long gone after all the kissing with Jason. He'd mentioned talking to me later when he dropped me off, but I wasn't sure what later meant to him. I wanted to text Marienne, but I didn't want to disturb her family time.

My family was spending time at my stepdad's brother's place, and Luke was studying and working. My father had died when I was five, so I'd grown up with Luke after our parents married when we were seven and twelve. He was pretty awesome as far as stepbrothers could go. Who wouldn't love a guy—as a brother, of course—who wanted to be a pediatrician? I was pretty sure most of my friends had crushes on him growing up, Phoebe for sure until she fell for our friend Sam.

I figured my mom would call me before too long to check in about the date. After the talk with Grammy, I was beginning to wish I'd never mentioned it. While my mother wasn't in any hurry to marry me off, Grammy worried she wouldn't live long enough to see me get married and wished it would happen sooner than later. Me being only eighteen seemed to matter very little in her desire for me to find a perfect mate.

At seventy-eight, Grammy had already outlived her husband, her only child (my father), and her sister and brother. I loved that she was active in her church and with her game club comprised almost entirely of ladies either a decade or two younger.

I wasn't even sure what type of games they played, except bridge, which I didn't understand. Grammy always seemed excited to host or attend the events. She'd embraced my stepdad and stepbrother as if they were her own and still considered my mother her "daughter-in-love" since families were forever. I could only hope I'd grow up to be like Grammy Pearl, or "Peach" to her friends.

After a shower, I halfway resembled a human. I got dressed in some shorts and a tank top and then stretched back out on my bed. There was no use trying to be productive on a Sunday afternoon. I discovered a text from Jason that was about ten minutes old.

Jason: U wanna hang later?

Me: I could probably hang. Want to grab food at the caf with me around 6? I know the food's not the greatest, but it is free with my extra meal swipes.

Jason: Free eats, good company, who am I to say no?

Me: Great. See you outside my dorm at 6.

Putting the phone back down, I wiped my palms on my shorts. He was easy to talk to, but damn, the boy made me nervous. And he thought I was good company. Was it the conversation or the making out he liked? Or both?

I woke up to the sound of someone knocking on my dorm window. A glance at my phone showed missed texts and calls from my mother and Jason. I'd left it on silent and fallen asleep again. It was a few minutes after six already. I got up and walked over to my window. When I peeked through the slats of the blinds, Jason was standing there. I raised the blinds and pushed open the window.

"Hey," he said as he popped the screen out of its frame.

"Sorry," I said, stepping back. "I fell asleep with my phone on silent."

Jason climbed through the window and approached me. I didn't know what to do, so I backed up until I crashed into my sink vanity. Jason laughed. "I figured it was something like that when you didn't answer."

"Let me grab my ID and then we can go eat." I glanced at my reflection in the mirror to make sure I didn't have crazy pillow creases on my face and Jason walked up behind me. He wrapped his arms around me and kissed the back of my neck, sending goosebumps all over my body. I turned to face him and let him kiss me while silently praying I didn't have nasty breath after sleeping again. If I did, he didn't seem to notice.

"Now I'm ready," he said, walking back to the window. He climbed out and reached back through to offer me his hand. "You coming?"

I sighed and shook my head at him before grabbing my keys and ID. Climbing out the dorm window was a first for me. At least it made living on the first floor a nice advantage despite all the noise and religious screaming coming from the room upstairs. It certainly made my virgin ears blush with the frequency in the two weeks since I'd moved in.

After a lackluster meal of rubbery pizza and soggy fries, Jason and I left the cafeteria and started walking away from my dorm. He wanted to show me something in the Art Building, so I went along with him, not sure if it counted as hanging out like he'd mentioned in his text earlier.

"I was surprised you didn't go home to see your family," Jason said. "Campus is usually pretty dead Labor Day weekend."

"My parents didn't want me on the road, and plus they're with my stepdad's brother's family anyway. My stepcousins are little hellions, so I'm not too disappointed to miss a barbeque where the two boys might shove me into the pool fully clothed. I had to get a new phone out of the incident last year."

"They were probably flirting with you—no blood relation—you know," he said with a chuckle. "Young teenagers, right?"

"No. Gross. And yes, they're thirteen and fifteen now, and they're asses to everyone. I've known them for over ten years, and I think they've been that way their whole lives."

"I don't have any cousins except Marienne. My mom's an only child, and my dad's only brother is Marienne's dad. My brother's twelve years older than me, so I became an uncle when I was still a teenager. I have two nieces who are pretty cute. They think I'm an awesome uncle since I buy them candy to sneak into the movies when I take them."

"I bet you're a fun uncle. No one's ever accused me of being too much fun, that's for sure."

"I bet you're more fun than you think."

"I appreciate you saying that. Guys in high school always thought I was too serious."

"And why is that?"

"Because I didn't wanna go to parties and get drunk off my ass every weekend."

"Well," Jason said with a smirk. "You could benefit from lightening up every now and then, even if it doesn't include getting drunk off your ass—and it's a mighty fine one too."

"Ugg, Jason!" I stopped walking as we reached the Art Building and could feel my face redden before he'd finished checking out my butt.

"What? Do I embarrass you by complementing your body?"

"A little. I don't exactly go around showing it off."

He laughed. "Well, maybe you should. You have a beautiful body."

"You haven't seen my body y—"

"Yet...meaning you might want to show it to me." He winked at me.

I sat down on the outdoor bench and buried my face in my hands. "God, Jason, could it be more obvious to you I'm an awkward virgin?"

He pulled me to my feet and kissed me on the forehead. "It's not a problem."

"I don't know if I'm ready for any of this."

"Well, I wasn't proposing we have sex right this moment...unless you want to, because I'm down for it."

"Jason!" I could feel blood rushing to my cheeks again and buried my face in his chest. Surely there had to be a limit on how many times I could blush in an evening. "I don't know you well enough yet."

"Does talking about sex embarrass you?"

"Another painfully obvious question," I muttered into his shirt. He smelled so good, like a mountain breeze with a hint of peppermint.

"Come on," Jason said as he grabbed my hand. He took his student ID card out of his wallet and swiped it to open the door. The door clicked open and then Jason led me inside.

Inside the printmaking lab Jason took me to a table on the far side of the room where several prints were laid out. It only took me half a second to realize all of the prints were of someone's butt. "Oh my..." I took a step back and covered my face with my hands.

Jason cracked up. "Do nude asses embarrass you too?"

"I wasn't expecting to see so many of them..." When I looked up again, Jason had dropped his pants, exposing his naked butt. "What are you doing?"

He looked over his shoulder and laughed as he pulled up his pants. "So, which is better? The original or all the copies?"

I started laughing at the absurdity of my situation. I'd seen nudity in art and movies, but I had never seen a guy naked in real life—something I was sure Jason had realized with my reaction to seeing part of him. I didn't know whether to be offended or keep laughing. "You're out of your mind! You used your own butt as a model for your art project?"

"I couldn't think of a finer specimen at the time...unless you're volunteering for my next round of prints."

My mouth dropped open, and Jason started laughing again. He walked over and rubbed my shoulders. "Like I said, Lydia, Lighten up a little!" He pulled me into a hug, further intoxicating me with his charm and incredible scent.

Soon we were kissing again right there in the printmaking classroom. There was a ferociousness in him, like he couldn't get enough of me. And I was starting to feel that way too as his tongue brushed against mine. It was definitely more than the chaste stage kissing I'd experienced before—this time with a person who actually wanted to kiss me, though I still wasn't sure why.

"So, why'd you ask me out?" I asked him in between kisses. "Marienne says you broke up with someone not too long ago."

Jason kissed me again. "I don't want to talk about my ex or my cousin."

"I'm curious about you and your past. I've never dated anyone before."

He sighed and leaned his head back. "I ended things because our relationship had run its course, and neither of us were happy. I needed to step back having to be with someone so I could focus on myself and school. I asked you out because I find you attractive, and I wanted to get to know you better. I'll turn the tables. Why did you agree to go out with me?"

"Same reasons, I guess. You seem interesting."

"Good to know," he said, taking my hand. "Come on, let's go for a walk. I feel like roaming around."

We walked and talked for hours, Jason showing me his favorite secret and secluded places on campus. I hadn't planned on pulling another all-nighter, but with Labor Day being the next day, it's not like I had anything else going on. Even if I'd had plans on Monday, I would have forgotten them in Jason's presence.

One moment he was showing me star constellations and the next he'd talk about Dante's *Inferno* and how it related to art. It was the most interesting conversation I'd ever had, hands down.

Then we talked about music and how a song could take you back to a moment like nothing else could. It didn't have to be a new song; it could be any song you associated with a moment. It was true. I adored music but unfortunately had no talent for playing it. My dad had been musically gifted, and my mom could sing, but Dad's talent had skipped over me. I'd tried piano and guitar lessons in the past, but both had proven too difficult or maybe I hadn't wanted it enough. At least I could sing for musicals, but there wouldn't be any record producers tripping over each other to sign me, and that was okay.

"Wow," I said as we stopped at a bench in the center of campus. "You have a lot going on inside that head of yours."

"Don't you?" he asked. "I bet you think about a lot of different things. What are you thinking about right now?"

"I'm wondering if Dante looked up at the same stars when he thought about his writing, and if Beethoven or Mozart were roamers like you. If Michelangelo searched for a perfect specimen when he carved the sculpture of David. You know...the standard thoughts of an eighteen-year-old."

Jason threw back his head and cackled. "See! I knew it. You're as weird as me, wondering about all those things. Now, I may not be as perfect of a specimen of a man as the model for the David, but I'll definitely let you see me in all my glory—when you're ready."

In the darkness, my red face didn't show, but I knew I'd be ready to see him soon, probably very soon in the grand scheme of time. He wrapped his arms around my waist and pulled me close again, kissing me gently on the forehead. It felt more intimate than any of our other kisses—so much that I felt dizzy.

"You keep mentioning taking off all your clothes and have already mooned me this evening. You're not secretly a nudist, are you?"

"I would never keep nudity a secret from you, Lydia," he said, pulling me by the hand. "Come on. Let's keep walking."

Eventually, we made it back to my dorm, and I let Jason in through my window. Even though very few people had stayed during the weekend, I was still too nervous to walk him through the lobby. I made it clear I had no intention of removing any clothing, and he agreed to keep his on as well as we laid together on my bed to watch a movie on my laptop.

He picked out some obscure comedy I tried to like, but I didn't get the humor of it. I made a point to laugh when Jason did. I understood what was meant to be funny, but I found it juvenile. I supposed I didn't have to love the same type of movies as him for us to get along.

Snuggling up next to him and feeling his warmth was enough for me as my mind wandered during the movie. Just being with him and listening to his heartbeat and the sound of his laughter as it burst from his chest was the best thing I could imagine.

It was what I'd been missing all that time. Male romantic companionship. I wanted so desperately to fall in love and have someone love me back. I was tired of feeling so lonely as friends talked about their boyfriends or girlfriends. I'd always longed for it too, but all of my crushes had been one-sided until Jason.

I knew Marienne and Vicki wouldn't come back to the dorms until late Monday evening to be ready for classes on Tuesday morning. I couldn't wait to tell them about my amazing weekend and hoped Marienne wouldn't be too weirded out by me dating her cousin because I wanted to keep seeing him.

But was it dating? Would I be able to consider Jason my boyfriend at some point in the future? I'd never had a boyfriend before—not a real one anyway. Handholding with the boy in kindergarten totally didn't count. Did Jason want me to be his girlfriend? Would asking him to declare his intentions for the relationship after only two dates scare him away? I had way too many questions and too many thoughts swirling around in my head.

Chapter 9
June 5, 2024

It's been a week since I visited the cemetery, and short of my time in the workshop, I haven't been able to get Jason off my mind. I keep replaying all our best and worst moments in my head—romanticizing things—as Phoebe says if I ever mention a memory to her.

Of course, I haven't told her I saw Jason again; I haven't told anyone. The people in my life who love me don't love Jason and would prefer to never hear his name leave my lips again.

Wednesdays are the only days off from the workshop, but I haven't told my parents, so I'll have time to make the trip to the cemetery each week. I can't stop looking over my shoulder constantly as I sit on the bench near Marienne's grave. I see the remains of the daffodils I left last time withered and dried beneath a newer bouquet of wildflowers. They look like the flowers Marienne's parents gave her at our college graduation. I remember how excited we both were with our upcoming plans to go to Europe soon after.

Two days after graduation, Marienne and I left the U.S. and spent almost two weeks overseas bouncing from London to Paris, Rome to Koblenz, and Brussels to Amsterdam. We came back with a lifetime of memories and then she was gone a few days later. It all happened so fast, and she was dead—killed instantly in a car crash. The other driver had died too, and no one knew who'd been at fault for the accident. And Jason disappeared from my life at the same time too, physically at least. He'd never left my mind.

I close my eyes and rest my head in my hands. I'm about to leave when I sense his presence near me. I uncover my eyes as I rise and turn to Jason. He gives me a close-mouthed smile.

"Hello again," he says.

"I was beginning to think you weren't coming."

"I'm here when you need me."

I sigh and roll my eyes. "That's a first. You developed quite the habit of disappearing on me when I needed you before."

"So, we're going to rehash the past again?"

"I guess so."

"I've apologized, Lydia. I don't know what else to do."

Despite how sincere he sounds I know I can't trust him again. He exhausted his chances long ago. But even after everything that happened between us, I still love him. I think he knows it.

"I don't know either," I say. "But you said you'd be ready to listen when I was ready to talk. I think I've practiced a hundred times what I'd say to you if I could, but now my mind is drawing a blank."

"I know I hurt you."

"Hurt me? Hurt me, Jason? You've got to be kidding me! What you did was so much more than hurt me. You devastated me. You shredded my heart into confetti and then threw the pieces all around, stomped all over them, and set them on fire for the hell of it."

He sits there biting his lip, so I continue. "You knew I was in love with you, and you didn't even have the guts to tell me to my face you were done with me."

"I told you I wasn't..."

"What. My boyfriend or boyfriend material at all? You think avoiding a stupid label prevents someone's heart from being broken? Call it whatever you want, just admit something actually happened between us."

"It's not about denial..."

"Isn't it?" I demand. "I seem to recall a conversation where you swore I was in denial about my feelings for you. What was it... 'projecting my ideals of a perfect relationship on you?' Like

I would ever describe the sum of all the parts of our 'fictitious relationship' as perfect."

"Maybe some of the individual parts by themselves?"

"Don't be a smart-ass."

"It's part of who I am."

"Maybe this isn't the time. I've got somewhere I need to be." I stand and walk away from him, calling back over my shoulder. "I may or may not see you next week."

When I get back to my car and look toward Marienne's grave, Jason is already gone. I realize it's the first time I've ever been the one to walk away from him and not the other way around.

Vicki's car is already in the parking lot when I arrive at the restaurant. Pulling up to *A Hole in the Wall* brings back memories of my first date with Jason, but I didn't want to spoil her trip through town by asking her to choose somewhere else to meet for lunch. Just because the place gives me heartburn—and I'm not talking about the food—doesn't mean Vicki can't love it.

I spot Vicki right away as I go inside. She waves frantically from the booth, even though she's only about three feet away from the front door, and then jumps up to hug me. It's been several months since we've seen each other in person. She's been busy finishing up her master's degree while substitute teaching to gain some experience. I'm amazed by how she took more than a full course load to complete her degree in only a year. But something I've learned about her is she packs a lot of determination into her small frame.

"Hey, girl!" she squeals. "Happy belated birthday! I've missed you so much! I have so much to tell you, and I wanted to share it in person!"

"It's good to see you too," I say, returning her hug. She's so tiny I feel like I could lift her off the ground while her arms are around my neck, but I don't.

After we order our burgers, we sit at the booth to wait, and the suspense is killing me. She's grinning so much her eyes are reduced to tiny slits. "Guess what?" she teases, a few of her red corkscrew curls escaping from her messy bun.

"Hmm, you've decided to forgo your teaching job and join the circus?"

"Ha!" she snorts. "Guess again!"

"You're moving to Korea to be a professional K-Pop groupie?"

"Nice! But no. I'm staying a little closer to home."

"Hmm, home, huh?" I knew she'd been offered a job at her old high school starting in August since one of her favorite history teachers had retired, so I knew she wouldn't give up the opportunity. "So, I guess that rules out running away to join the circus."

"I am moving out of my parents' house soon, though."

"So, you found an apartment? I'll have to admit I'm a little let down by the news..."

"Oh my gosh, Lydia! Denton proposed! We're getting married! The last weekend in July before I have to get ready to teach full time. I want you to be my maid of honor!" She squeals again, shoving her left hand in my face to show me a diamond much too large for her tiny finger.

Pain grips my stomach like a vise. "That's great, Vicki! And so soon. I'm really happy for you and Denton! Of course, I'll be your maid of honor."

A worker at the counter calls our order number and Vicki jumps up to get it. I take a deep breath to compose myself and try to focus on the amazing aroma of our food as she places it in front of me.

"I almost spilled the beans when we talked on the phone yesterday!" Vicki continues, chomping on a fry. "I've been waiting to announce it on Instagram until after I could ask you to be in the wedding. I'm having my two cousins be junior bridesmaids, so it will be so much fun! With the leftover spring décor at the church, we won't have to spend much on that stuff, and I'll make sure your dress is something you can wear again. I'm thinking something tea-length in light green, what do you think? It will really bring out your eyes! And my dress will be white, of course, but with a green sash to tie in the color. And I'm hoping no one thinks it's a typo when we list everything as the Price-Pierce wedding..."

My mind wanders a bit as Vicki spills the other details of her dream wedding. I'm happy for her and Denton, I really am. They've been together since junior high, but of course, it's also another reminder of how alone I feel. It's hard to be ecstatic for my friend and also devastated by my own selfish feelings at the same time.

"So how have you been?" Vicki asks. "How's the workshop? Met anyone interesting there?"

"It's good so far. There's a guy named Kolton who seems pretty nice. We've been paired off to do some of the practice scenes together."

"Is he cute?"

I laugh. "Yeah, but I'm not thinking of romance right now, but I think we're on the way to becoming good friends."

"Being friends is good. It's how Denton and I started out. You never know, and you can never have too many friends."

"Speaking of that, I went to the cemetery today."

Vicki leans across the table and places her hand over mine, her engagement ring sparkling in the light. "I know it's awful for you since you and Marienne were so close. Plus, everything with

Jason. That must have been hard That's the first time you've been since the funeral, right?"

"Actually, I went last Wednesday for the first time while I was in town. It's a bit easier now since more time has passed. I can go and talk about what's on my mind."

She squeezes my hand. "You can always talk to me too, day or night, anytime. I hate it I wasn't able to be there with you that day...or when you felt the worst." Vicki had been out of town on a cruise with her parents and Denton's family when the accident happened. She'd come to my parents' house as soon as she was back and sat with Phoebe and me for hours while I cried. I barely remember the passage of time after the funeral. And the week after—when all the initial shock had worn off—was even harder.

"I know. But enough about me and my broken heart, tell me every detail about how Denton proposed."

Vicki gives me a play-by-play, and it's just as I suspected. Super cheesy and romantic—exactly right for her. He'd hired a sky-writer plane to spell out his proposal over the field near the school where their eighth-grade dance was held as he took her on a backward tour of significant places in their love history. I hate being jealous of her happiness and I feel like a terrible person since I'd rather be anywhere else in the world right now.

Thankfully, Vicki starts talking about her classes next and I'm able to clamp down my jealousy and give her the full attention she deserves while we finish eating.

As I leave the restaurant, I take a sudden detour to the road that leads to a lookout point. I haven't been there since Jason took me five years ago, but the place is tugging at my heartstrings all the same. When I pull up, I'm relieved to find it deserted because my whole soul is about to break apart with all the emotions I've held back. I park myself on the rock wall and let it all out, sobbing into my hands. My pulse is racing, and I feel dizzy, so I lie back to catch my breath.

When my phone rings later, I realize an hour has passed and Phoebe's calling.

"Hey, girl," I answer.

"I wanted to make sure you'd made it home. I thought you were going to call me."

"I'm sorry. I got held up a little longer after lunch with Vicki. Guess what? Denton proposed and they're getting married at the end of July!"

"That's great, news, Lyds, but how do you feel about it?"

Damn it. She always knows. "I'll be fine. I'm going to be her maid of honor, and we both know Denton's a great guy. They're the type of couple who will be together forever."

"I know, but I also know you, and I can tell you've been crying."

"I promise, I'll be fine. I went to the cemetery today too, so I'm a little more emotional than usual."

Phoebe sighs. "I don't want you to keep hurting yourself by going there."

"It hurts no matter where I am, Phoebe." Part of me regrets having told her about the first visit last week.

"That's not what I mean. I mean you can talk to the people you lost anytime you want without having to go to their graves two weeks in a row. You don't visit your dad's grave much, and it's near your parents' house. Driving so far out of your way seems like you're punishing yourself. And you shouldn't do that. The accident wasn't your fault."

"I had business in town both days, Phoebe. I needed my notarized college transcript for the workshop so I can claim graduate credit, and then today I was meeting Vicki because she happened to be stopping by the college. I'm not planning to make a habit of going to the cemetery every Wednesday, not that I should have to explain myself."

"Lydia, I miss you. We need to spend some time together this weekend, okay?"

"I have to work until nine on Friday and Saturday night."

"Then we'll go to a late movie on Saturday. I'm not taking 'no' for an answer this time."

"Fine. I'll see you Saturday. Bye."

I love Phoebe, but I can't tell her I'm talking to Jason again any more than I can tell Vicki. I can't talk to anyone I know about him. My friends and family saw what losing him twice had done to me, and no one would understand my need for more closure. Being crushed via email the first time had felt pretty final at the time, and the cruelty of it had shattered me. I forgave him and we got back together for a while, but things had ended again—forever this time.

I'm not even sure what I want from him now since there's no turning back. Some days I want a heartfelt apology and other days I want him to tell me he's always loved me despite his awful way of showing it. I want him to tell me he was wrong to leave me and he's miserable without me.

Often, I wish I lived in a place and time where he could take me in his arms and truly make love to me because no one ever touched me like that before I let him, and no one has since. The thought of someone else touching me makes my skin crawl despite how lonely I feel sometimes.

I wonder which condition will prove fatal first, the loneliness or the heartache?

Chapter 10
September 2, 2019

I slept late on Labor Day and wondered what the afternoon would hold for me. Jason had stayed until early morning and left without us making any definite plans. I hoped he'd call or text me later, but everything was still too new to know what he might do. I didn't remember him saying anything about plans with his family, but it wouldn't be strange for them to have a barbeque like lots of other families.

All I could do was hang out in the dorm after lunch because I didn't want to drive around town by myself. I wanted so badly to text Jason or call him to see what he was doing, but that might come across as pushy or needy. Ugh, dating was hard!

I picked up *On the Road* by Jack Kerouac at least three different times in between watching funny videos on my phone, but my mind couldn't focus long enough to comprehend what I was reading. I'd have to get to it within the next two weeks for my literature class, but daydreaming about Jason didn't mesh well with the original scroll and its lack of punctuation and structure.

Finally, I settled on some bad reality TV and dozed throughout the afternoon. I didn't hear anything from Jason.

When Marienne and Vicki got back to the dorms on Monday evening, we went to the cafeteria for dinner. I felt like a different person than I'd been three days before. Spending all that time with Jason made me truly understand what I'd been missing by not dating in high school.

I mean, I knew I wanted a boyfriend, but I had never understood how truly lonely I'd been until I had something real to miss. Some*one* real. And after only a day apart, I already missed Jason. I was lost in my thoughts as we sat at our usual table in the cafeteria and realized Marienne and Vicki were sitting across from me staring, neither of them eating yet.

"Okay, spill it," Marienne said. "What did you do all weekend stuck here on campus?"

I could feel myself blushing. "I went out on a date with Jason."

"That's great!" Vicki said.

"Eww!" Marienne said at the same time. "Gross. I can't comprehend anyone wanting to date my idiot cousin. He's the worst possible boyfriend candidate out there as far as I'm concerned."

"Well, you're not supposed to want to date your cousin, girl!" Vicki exclaimed.

"I know that! I just don't want to see Lydia get hurt! Jason can be selfish and full of himself sometimes—no, scratch that—all the time."

"Excuse me, don't I have a say in who I choose to date?" I asked.

Marienne sighed. "Please be careful and make sure you communicate with him about what you need. Otherwise, he'll be all caught up in himself like he's always been."

"You think I'm naïve, don't you?" I asked Marienne.

"I love my cousin, but I don't like the way he seems to send mixed signals to girls."

"Ouch," Vicki said. "I've known guys like that. They're scum if they can't be honest about their intentions."

"I'll be careful," I promise. "I'm getting to know him right now."

"Which is fine if you're in it for fun," Marienne relented. "Remember to guard your heart."

Of course, maybe what she really meant was I wasn't good enough or mature enough for him to fall in love with me. I looked down at my soggy fries and dragged them through the ketchup on my tray.

"I'm sorry, Lydia," Marienne said. "It's nothing against you. Jason hasn't been mature enough to let someone truly love him, nor has he shown the capacity to love someone back. And honestly, I think you're too good for him."

"Well, people change all the time," Vicki interjected, trying to lighten the mood. "I've got your back, girl. And if Jason doesn't treat you right, Denton will teach him some manners."

"And to warn you, Lydia, Jason's not the 'saving himself for marriage' type, if that hasn't already come up," Marienne said.

"I'm saving myself for love, so I don't think it'll be a problem if what you say about Jason is true," I said. "Besides, he hasn't texted me all day after we spent the past two days together, so maybe you're right and he's already dropping me."

Marienne sighed and reached across the table to pat my hand.

Vicki patted my other hand, sharing grease from the pepperoni pizza she'd been eating. "Give it time," she said. "Don't seem too eager, and he'll come around if it's meant to be."

Marienne groaned as she picked up her tiny carton of chocolate milk. "Love stinks."

There had to be more to the story than her disdain for her cousin's love life. Perhaps she'd been hurt badly by love and wanted to save others from the risk. I figured I'd learn more soon and decided not to pry.

Later, in our room, Marienne sprawled out on her bed and stared at the ceiling while I read some lines aloud for our theatre class. She responded to me without having to look at her notes, and I was impressed she'd already memorized the lines over the weekend.

"I guess you had plenty of time to study, huh?"

"Not really," she said, turning toward me. "Having a photographic memory helps with lines."

"You suck so much! I have to run lines dozens of times before I get them."

She grinned. "I can't help it. I'm gifted in that area. Don't worry, I know you'll be fabulous on Broadway someday. Trust me; I know these things."

"What about you? Do you want Broadway too, or are you going for Hollywood, lady?"

"I know I'd like to be famous in one way or another, if not infamous. Who knows? I've always had an easier time seeing other people's futures. Mine draws a blank when I think about life after college."

"Probably because it's too amazing to imagine right now."

"I hope so. That's what Corey said when we were together, but it didn't end well."

"I'm sorry to hear that."

"It's fine. One ex-girlfriend in a sea of millions of people isn't going to keep me down forever. Broken hearts have a tendency to heal. Eventually."

"Oh. I didn't know Corey was a ... well, I didn't know you dated women."

"I've dated a lot—guys, girls, non-binary—it doesn't matter to me. Corey was special though, and the first time I was in an exclusive relationship. I thought we'd make it, but she didn't want to do the long-distance thing, and it was too hard to stay friends. We were together a little over a year."

"Wow, that's a long time."

"Yeah, but like that old song says, 'Sometimes love ain't enough.' Unless you're someone like Vicki where it is. She's the kind of person whose whole life will be filled with rainbows and unicorn farts. People like you and me, we have to suffer a bit to get our happiness. It's the way of the serious actor."

I laughed and tossed my notes at her. "I don't plan to suffer too much!"

"I hope you don't." She picked up her phone off the nightstand, started texting someone, and then my phone dinged.

When I picked it up, I had to smile.

Marienne: I love you. Will you be my best friend forever and always?

Me: Try and stop me.

My Tuesday morning classes seemed to drag on forever, and Vicki checked to make sure I was okay as my knee bounced during our math class. I wanted to see Jason again and since we didn't share any classes, and I didn't want to seem too desperate by texting him, I knew I'd have to wait until our Art Club meeting.

I barely waited for our instructor to assign homework before I bailed out of my desk and left for the Art Building, calling out a goodbye to Vicki. I got to the building out of breath and took a minute to compose myself before heading upstairs. I was the first to arrive, so I chose a seat facing the door to see Jason when he came in. I hoped we'd get a minute alone to catch up before the others showed up.

It was several minutes after the scheduled meeting start time before anyone else strolled in, as usual. Other members came in and greeted me as I stared at the door and listened for Jason's footsteps. Soon I heard voices in the hallway and recognized Jason's laugh at something Nora was saying as they walked into the room. Nora's mohawk was combed down, and she was wearing a baby doll dress with combat boots. Jason was grinning ear to ear as he sat on top of the table at the front of the room. I hoped he'd at least greet me, but he didn't.

"Greetings, fellow club members," he said. "I trust everyone had a good holiday weekend. Mine was quite relaxing."

He didn't even glance my way, and I could feel bile rising in my throat.

"Nora and I were talking about the carnival that's coming up this Thursday, and she's got all the paint and new brushes. Be sure to get with Lydia to sign up for at least a thirty-minute shift during the event. Nora still has the stencils from last year for those of you who are better at sculpture or graphic design than drawing or painting, so it should be easy participation points."

They hadn't spoken to me about creating a sign-up sheet for the meeting, so I quickly made one while Jason rambled on about how last year's carnival had gone and the ways we could make it more fun. I added my name to a couple of slots and then passed around the sheet for the other members to do so. I'd never painted faces before but figured it wouldn't be too hard with stencils. Besides, I knew a lot of the students would be drinking before the event anyway and wouldn't know the difference between good and bad facial décor.

When the meeting ended, everyone left but Jason, Nora, and me. I walked over to them to share the list of volunteers. I stepped a little closer to Jason and brushed against his arm as I placed the paper on the table in front of us. He moved away.

"Looks like all the slots are full," I said. "Jason, there's one slot where I'm working alone, and I could use help if you're planning to take a slot."

"Great job, Lydia," Nora said. "I think you'll be fine in the first slot since a lot of students don't arrive until later."

Jealousy raced through my veins, and I didn't like it one bit. "Thank you, Nora, but I was asking Jason since I figured he'd want to put in an appearance as president of Art Club. You've already signed up for two slots."

Jason cleared his throat. "I'll be at the carnival the whole time, so I'll stop in and check on all the shifts and lend a hand when I need to. Will you send Nora and me a copy of the list? You've got both of our numbers, right?"

"Well, you already know I have yours. Nora?"

Nora handed me a business card with an illustration of some red and black art on the front. "Here you go, Lydia," she said. "All my info's there. See you Thursday!"

After she left, I turned back to Jason and walked closer, hoping he'd touch me. He was busy shuffling through some papers in a locker at the back of the room.

"I hope you had a good Labor Day," I said.

"Yeah, did you?"

"It was good. I hung out by myself and did some reading for class." I brushed his arm again and he backed away like I'd burned him.

"You're kinda crowding me here," he said softly as another art student came into the room.

"Fine," I said, gritting my teeth. "See you." My jaw started aching as I left the room and I managed to make it to the restroom stall before everything spilled over. I hadn't expected him to treat me so coldly after such a nice weekend. What the hell was going on? Was he having second thoughts about seeing me? Had I done something wrong?

"I don't want to say, 'I told you so,' but I did tell you Jason can be an asshole," Marienne said later that evening as I curled up on my bed with a death grip on my huge yellow teddy bear.

"I don't get it. What did I do? He treated me like a stranger and then said I was crowding him when I stood too close."

"You didn't do anything wrong, Lydia," she said. "It's him."

"But..."

"I know. He made you feel special over the weekend, but he's not good boyfriend material for you or anyone else. Try not to think about him and focus on your classes."

"It's not that easy."

She got up and sat beside me on the bed, smoothing my hair behind my ears. "I know, and I can't promise I won't kick him in the junk next time I see him for hurting your feelings."

I laughed. "Please don't."

I didn't talk to Jason or text him at all while I waited for carnival day. I couldn't stop thinking about him, though. I knew I had to have done something wrong. Maybe he wasn't good with public displays of affection, and I'd made him uncomfortable. That had to be it. I'd wait and talk to him alone and then we could work everything out.

No one was at the face painting booth when I got there, but all the paint and supplies were sitting on the folding table. I sat down and waited as other students started arriving. The first customer was a tall guy with thick, curly black hair I recognized from two of my classes.

"Hey. Lydia, right?" he said, taking the chair across from me.

"Yeah, we have Freshman Comp and Intro to Theatre together. Cameron, right?"

"Yup, I'm Cameron. Can you paint a moon and sun on my cheeks? The top ones."

At least my flushing top cheeks could be blamed on the heat outside. "Thanks for clarifying," I told him as I shuffled through the stencils. "I'll get you fixed up in no time."

I didn't have a clue what I was doing, but halfway through painting the moon, I could feel someone watching me from afar. As I turned, Jason looked away and kept walking by like he was on a mission. I turned back to Cameron. "So why a moon and a star? Any significance?"

"A moon and a *sun*, but a star would be cool too. It's how my mom decorated my room when I was a kid. I've always liked astronomy and astrology too, for that matter. What's your sign?"

"Aren't you supposed to ask what my major is first? This isn't the 1960s."

"Fine, what's your major? And what's your sign?"

"I'm majoring in Theatre Arts, and I'm a Gemini."

"Ooh, the twins. A mysterious woman."

"What about you?"

"Speech Communication and minoring in Theatre. Scorpio."

"Nice."

"Can I ask you something?"

I picked up a new paintbrush to start on the sun. "Haven't you been asking me things already?"

Before Cameron could answer, Jason walked up and took a seat. "How's it going here? You have enough paint?" he asked.

"Everything's good," I said. "Cameron is my first victim."

"I'll confess," Cameron said. "I'm only getting my face painted because I wanted to ask Lydia out."

My heart started pounding so hard I could feel it in my gut. It hadn't occurred to me that Cameron liked me.

Jason stood up and pushed in his chair. "Well, I gotta head out," he said. "Later."

I turned back to Cameron and put the finishing touches on the moon design. "I think we're done here," I told him, handing him the mirror. "Will that do?" The design looked awful, I had to admit.

Cameron grinned. "Looks like a face painting," he said. "So...I was wondering if you'd maybe want to hang out sometime. Like go see a movie or bowling or something like that?"

I took a deep breath. "I'm seeing someone right now, but thanks for the offer. We can hang out as friends sometime. I'll see you in class."

He frowned and then smiled at me. "Well, at least I worked up the nerve to ask. Thanks, Lydia. I'd like to be friends. See ya later."

As flattered as I was that Cameron had asked me out, the whole situation made me feel queasy, and Jason's behavior hadn't helped. Was he jealous?

Nora showed up to take over after I'd painted flowers on the faces of at least a dozen sorority girls. Their enthusiasm didn't match my mood, and I was tired of hiding it. Nora said she couldn't get ahold of Jason and gave me the keys to her locker in the Art Building to go get the rest of the paint. I was thrilled to have a task that didn't involve faking a smile even if it meant trekking halfway across campus as it was getting dark.

Jason's truck was parked in the loading zone in front of the Art Building. I took a deep breath as I went inside, silently praying I wouldn't run into him and also hoping I would. When I got to the second-floor classroom where Nora's locker was, Jason stood above a table with several prints spread out on it. He looked up at me and smiled when I walked in. I didn't have the strength to smile at him, so I gave him a wide berth and walked straight to Nora's locker to get the paint. When I turned around with the bag in my hand, Jason was standing behind me, super close.

I backed into the locker and looked up at him. "What's up?" he asked.

"You're kinda crowding me," I snapped, walking around him.

He moved to the other side of me and stood in front of the door. "Lydia, don't be like that."

"Don't be like what, an asshole? *You* seem pretty good at it."

He looked down and then tried to touch my arm, but I backed away. "I guess I deserve that. I should have called or texted, but I've been busy this week dealing with some shit."

"What's up with you?"

"Dr. Ramiro said all my prints are mediocre, so I need to up my game if I'm going to pass my senior project."

I felt a little sorry for him. "I'm sorry to hear that, but you don't have to take it out on me. You were extremely rude. I didn't expect you to hold my hand in front of everyone during the meeting, but you didn't have to treat me like a stranger either."

"I'm not big on PDA."

"It's not like I tried to sit in your lap or kiss you. I just stood a bit too close apparently and you were a jerk about it. It hurt my feelings."

Jason sighed and pulled me in for a hug. How could I not melt at the show of affection? "I didn't mean to hurt your feelings."

"It's okay, just try not to do it again."

"So, do you wanna go out with the guy whose face you painted so terribly?" he asked with a chuckle. I pulled away and looked up at him as he smirked.

"You've got to be kidding me," I said, pushing him away with a laugh. "I gotta get this paint to Nora. We'll talk more later, okay? Will you still be here?"

"Yeah, okay," he said as I walked away. I think we both knew I'd be back. I couldn't stay away for long since the air felt magnetized between us.

I went back to the Art Building after the carnival and spent two hours making out half-naked with Jason in the darkroom. I wasn't ready to go all the way yet, but it would be sooner than later the way I was feeling about him. Every touch woke areas in my body I'd never noticed before.

Chapter 11
June 6, 2024

In addition to our conversations at the cemetery, Jason's visiting me in my sleep too. If getting over him is even possible, I've got to find a way to stop the dreams. When I'm asleep, we're happy. We're together. Marienne is alive and well, and all is right in my world.

But awake, staring at the ceiling in my parents' house, I know I have to get out of here soon. I can't get better and keep existing with my heartache when I feel trapped in my childhood bedroom—and in a version of myself I don't know or recognize anymore.

Realistically, I can't justify moving out right now since my current part-time job hours won't cover rent. Especially since my hours were cut so I could attend the workshop. I have inheritance money from my grandmother, but I want to save it for my eventual move to New York or the months of living on the road if I get a part in the play.

I drag myself to the shower where I cry what tears I can spare, hoping to still have some left for the workshop. I know we'll be working on crying exercises today. I'm afraid if I don't pre-cry then I might not be able to stop when the director ends the scenes.

I've never once missed a dose of my antidepressants, but even so, I feel dark clouds creeping in. Perhaps next Wednesday I should visit my therapist instead of Jason at the cemetery. But I know I can't stop seeing him. Not yet. I'm an addict and Jason is my drug. There's no use trying to deny my feelings. Despite how many times he's hurt me and left me behind, I still love him. I always will.

Kolton is all smiles when I sit down beside him at the workshop. I can't help but return his smile; his enthusiasm is contagious.

"It's good to see you again, Lydia," he says. "I hope you had a good day off. You ready to bring on some tears today?"

"It was good, and I think I can manage to get a little weepy today," I say. "How about you? You well rested and ready to go?"

"You won't think I'm less manly when I cry better than anyone?"

"Oh, I don't think there's a danger of me finding you less manly..." I tease.

"Ouch," he says, holding his heart. "That cut deep enough to make me cry right now."

We both laugh as Bernetta blows her whistle to get everyone's attention.

"Pair up, everyone, same partners from before!" she shouts. "I want you all to be ready for crying in fifteen!" She runs around thrusting scripts at everyone, and by that time, Kolton and I have wordlessly communicated our enthusiasm. I've definitely gained a new friend.

Kolton and I are the last group to perform, and my emotions are already running high with the memories of my dreams versus the reality of my life. After a playful game of "rock, paper, scissors," fate decides Kolton will make me cry first. I take a deep breath and walk to the center of the stage with him trailing behind me. We've decided to use our real names to make things easier for now.

"Hey, Lydia," Kolton says. "Thank you for coming in today."

"You didn't give me much choice, Dr. Black," I tell him, wringing my hands for the effect. "You said it was urgent, so here I am. What's going on?"

"Well, I'm sorry to have to tell you this, so I'll just say it. Luke's gone. There's nothing anyone could have done."

"What are you talking about? Luke can't be gone. My brother is young and healthy! You told me he'd be okay once he woke up!" I cross the stage to stand in front of Kolton.

"I'm so sorry, Lydia. He died this morning."

I slam my open hands against Kolton's chest, and he lets himself fall backward a bit as I burst into tears. Our classmates gasp. "You shouldn't lie to people!"

"I didn't mean to, I promise." Kolton wraps his arms around me and speaks into my ear. "You're going to be okay."

I jerk away from Kolton and hastily wipe my face. "I don't believe you!"

"Cut!" shouts Bernetta. "Great job!"

Kolton grins at me and hands me a pack of travel tissues. After I wipe my face, we're ready to work again. He comes rushing in from the side and frantically looks around. "Doctor! I need to see the doctor in charge!"

I approach him with my arms held out in a calming motion. "Sir, I'm going to need you to calm down. What can I do for you?"

"I won't calm down! My sister. Kendra Black. Where is she? She's been in an accident."

"Come with me, Mr. Black," I say, attempting to lead him by the arm.

Kolton jerks away. "No! Not until someone tells me what the hell's going on!"

I sigh and lower my head. "Mr. Black, I'm so sorry, but Kendra's injuries were extensive. We did everything we could to revive her, but our efforts didn't work. Kendra died from her injuries."

Kolton brings his hand over his mouth to cover a choked sob as tears run down his cheeks, then he drops to his knees and falls to the floor, his body shaking. "No, no, no!" he cries. "That's not possible." His last lines are barely a whisper before Bernetta interrupts with loud clapping.

"That's how it's done, folks," she says as Kolton stands up and wipes his eyes with a tissue, shooting a wink my way.

Our classmates clap for us as we return to our seats. I close my eyes for a moment to collect myself and imagine being backstage at a large production, and then I feel a hand in mine. I open my eyes to Kolton and squeeze his hand. I'm not sure what will happen with the workshop, but I want to know him better. The whole thing makes me uneasy.

Later, we break for lunch, and I pile into Kolton's car along with Nel and Tom. Tanya and Jake plan to meet us at the diner. It feels good to be around theatre people again. Though none of us are couples, we've been paired off for the play and know there's no guarantee any of us will get a part, much less the lead roles. Even so, we all agree over club sandwiches to support each other's work and not get too competitive. It isn't worth it with everything we've all been through.

"I'm glad to have weird people to talk to again," Tom says, polishing off the last of his sandwich. "My family is too normal, and it crushes my soul a bit each time I hold back my strangeness."

"Speak for yourself, Tom," Nel teases. "I'd like to officially label you as the only weirdo in the group."

"Here, here!" Tanya says.

Tom turns to Kolton, Jake, and me. "Dudes, help me out, please. Can we all just be who we are?"

"I don't know if I'm emotionally ready to answer that question after seeing everyone here cry their eyes out today," Kolton says.

Jake spews out a laugh that seems to erupt out of him. "Kolton, man, you took the cake on the blubbering today! No one else dropped to their knees like you!"

"What can I say," Kolton says, stroking his non-existent chin hair. "I've always been an overachiever. Full of the acting spirit."

"You're full of something..." I say.

"Me thinks the lady speaks of truth!" Tom says, and we all join in the laughter.

It feels good to have found my people again, and I can tell they feel the same as we fall into effortless conversation until it's time to return to the workshop.

By the end of the day, I'm both exhausted and invigorated from all the crying and running lines with Kolton, so when he asks me to grab a burger with him after the workshop, I don't hesitate to join him. We agree to meet each other there, and only on the way do I worry it's a date. Even though we haven't been together in a long time—or ever according to Jason—I still feel like I'm cheating on him as I park beside Kolton.

As we sit down with our burgers and fries, Kolton grins at me. "What?" I ask. "Do I have something stuck in my teeth already?"

"No," he says. "I'm happy to be hanging out with the woman who's gonna get the lead role in the production."

I can feel myself blushing. "That's not a given."

"You were incredible today, Lydia. I've never seen anyone get into the part as much as you did."

"I think you were the incredible one, but so was everyone else. Everyone in the workshop is really talented. Even though we made a pact with the others to not be competitive, you have to admit there's some steep competition."

"I'm allowed to have a favorite."

"Whatever," I say, shaking my head.

"Tell me more about yourself."

"What's there to tell?" I ask, taking a bite of my burger.

"Childhood, college, favorite color...the basics."

I finish chewing and swallow. "I grew up on the outskirts of Benton, went to Russellville for college, and have always had an affinity for red. You?"

"I can't let you off too easily. Elaborate, please."

I sigh. "Fine. I didn't think there'd be a quiz."

It's easy to open up to Kolton about my dad dying when I was little, and my mom remarrying my stepdad, Larry. I tell him all about Luke and his residency at St. Jude in Tennessee.

Kolton tells me about his love of Harrison Ford movies and his desire to have film roles in the future in addition to keeping up with live acting. He'd grown up outside of Little Rock and had chosen Fayetteville for college to be at his parents' alma mater. He wished he'd taken more theatre classes while getting his communications degree.

I'd chosen my college because they'd offered me a full scholarship, and I wanted to get through school without a lot of debt.

"Sometimes I regret not going farther away from home for college," I say to Kolton, who smiles as he listens to me. "Other times I know it was the right place to be at the time."

"Because of your friend?"

"Yeah. I miss her, but I wouldn't have met Marienne if I hadn't chosen the path I did. Of course, I wouldn't have met her cousin Jason either and let him break my heart, but that's another story entirely."

"I'm sorry." Kolton drags a fry through a mixture of ketchup and mustard and then pops it in his mouth. "I can't say much about healing heartache. I mean, I already told you I swore off dating for a long time. I'm just now getting to a place where I think I can move forward with someone else. Someday, anyway."

"I get it. Loneliness is better than the uncertainty of ever finding someone again and sometimes..."

"It gets almost unbearable. After I caught Maisy cheating on me with Mason, my former best friend, I lost two people I loved all at once. Our other friends were torn between taking sides with them or me, so I told them all not to bother and walked away. I can't be sure who knew and who didn't since they'd been screwing around for about six months."

"That long? Why not end it with you first?"

"That's what I said too. I'll never understand the compulsion to cheat."

"Me neither." And having been on the receiving end—sort of, since Jason and I weren't technically together—I know how much it hurts.

Kolton nods as he mixes more mustard and ketchup. He winks after catching me watching him. "I know, it seems gross, but don't knock it until you try it." He holds out a fry to me.

I take it and give it a try, and as I expected, it's terrible. "That's disgusting," I say, grabbing my water to wash it down. "You owe me some details about your life after forcing me to eat that abomination of condiments."

Kolton's the baby in the family since Kendra is a whole three minutes older, and she never lets him forget it. Their parents have been married for thirty years and still hold hands when they walk, and he still catches them making out sometimes. He loves them but understands why Kendra has kept her distance since coming out when they were teens. Especially since they stayed at the church where some of the members were so cruel to his sister. Kolton left the church too, but his parents still try to get him to go back.

"I just can't, so we agree to disagree," Kolton explains, wringing his hands. "I know God understands."

He speaks with confidence, but his body language tells me a different story. I think part of him still misses the church even if it wasn't the best place for him. I know how it feels to miss something (or someone) not good for you. "I've never attended church on a regular basis. I went with my grandma sometimes when I was a kid after my dad died, but it's never been a big part of my life."

"He's not the church. God, I mean. I think some of the best people have probably never set foot inside a church. And there are so many different interpretations of the Bible. It's a beautiful piece of literature, but I'm not sure everything in it was meant to be taken literally."

"I'd have to agree with you on the parts I've read. I should probably read the whole thing at some point."

"Only if you feel compelled to do so. I don't think knowing the Bible cover to cover is a requirement to get to the afterlife."

I think of Marienne and close my eyes, soaking in the moment. "I hope not."

"Do you want to talk about your friend?" Kolton asks. "No pressure."

I look at him and have a feeling I can tell him anything, so I do. I talk about Marienne and how losing her will haunt me forever. I tell him about falling in love with Jason only to have him break my heart in the end. Of course, I don't say a word about talking to Jason again in the cemetery because I still have the need to keep a secret only for myself.

Before I know it, hours have passed and we're still talking over cold fries and sweating drinks. Kolton glances at his watch and groans.

"I've kept you too long…"

"It's not that," he says. "My parents are out of town, so I have to go let their dog out. I need to get going."

We gather our trash and throw it away as we leave the burger place. Right before Kolton gets to his car, I call out to him.

"What is it?" he asks, half in and half out of his car.

"Don't think I'll let you go without you telling me your favorite color!"

He laughs. "Bright yellow." Just like sunshine.

I watch as he gets in his car and drives away before dropping into my car. While it wasn't a date, being with someone without all the pressure to be an old version of myself was refreshing and is exactly what I need.

I manage to keep my secret from Phoebe when we go out on Saturday night. She's interested in the workshop, so I'm able to fill my conversation time with tales of all the new people I've met. Of course, she is most interested in hearing more about Kolton, so I indulge her without mentioning he and I had talked about our exes more than we'd considered a date in the future.

Phoebe still swoons over Sam like they've just met despite having known each other practically forever, and I envy her for that. He's working full time while Phoebe gets her master's degree in teaching. I'm not surprised Phoebe's never wavered on what she wanted to be since she was six years old. I don't love kids enough to ever consider teaching, not that I hate them; I just prefer the company of people older than eighteen most of the time.

It's funny how both of my best friends now, Phoebe and Vicki, are teachers. I feel like watching them both in their relationships is teaching me what a healthy one is supposed to look like.

Chapter 12
September 28, 2019

I never thought my lips could feel swollen and bruised from so much kissing, but that's exactly how they felt during the weeks after Jason and I had our first minor argument. Since then, he'd been super attentive when we were alone, and we'd spent a couple of hours each night making out and talking in one of our vehicles or in a locked room in the Art Building.

Jason wanted to have sex with me, but he took my answer of "soon" as a good enough reason to wait. Each time he touched me, though, I wanted to wait less and less. The only thing that stopped us one Friday night was the fact I'd started my period (and my new prescription for birth control pills from the County Health Department) and told him it wasn't a good time for his hands to go exploring below my pants.

We still had a nice time fooling around since Marienne had gone home for the weekend to work. I didn't tell any of my friends how far we'd gone because it felt special having a secret between the two of us.

When I finally went home to visit my parents, I worried my mother would see right through me the moment I walked through the door, and I was right.

After hugging me, Mom grinned and held me out at arm's length. "So...tell me about the boy you've been seeing," she said.

"I've already told you about Jason over the phone," I said, reaching for the laundry bag I'd dropped inside the front door.

She followed me to the laundry room. "But I can tell by looking at you that you're smitten. Is he being a gentleman?"

"Of course," I said, my cheeks burning while I loaded the washer. "We're still getting to know each other, not planning a wedding or courting 1800s style."

Mom followed me to my bedroom and sat on the end of my bed as I looked through my closet for some fall clothes to take back with me. "I want you to remember your values, Lydia."

She meant her values. "I know. I don't have to do anything I don't want to do."

"Just don't give in to pressure from this guy. Sex is not a requirement when you're dating someone."

"Geez, Mom! I'm not having sex with him! We barely know each other!"

"Well, I waited until my wedding night with your father, and I'm glad I did."

I cringed, having heard the story since puberty too many times to count. I never asked if Dad had also waited, and I didn't want to know. While my mother preached abstinence over anything, she still told me with great detail everything that could happen if I chose differently.

"Pregnancy is always a possibility even with protection, remember that."

"Mom, please," I begged. "I don't need the sex talk again. I'm still recovering from the first one and all the other times we've talked about it."

"Well, if you're too embarrassed to talk about it, then you're too young to be doing it."

"I'm not embarrassed!" I was mortified. "It's just unnecessary. I know all the benefits of abstinence and all the ways to protect myself otherwise."

"Never hurts to have a refresher. I know you're an adult at eighteen, and you're old enough to make your own decisions, but my sweet girl, you're also young enough to get seriously hurt. I don't want to see that happen."

I walked over to my bed and sat down beside her. "I know." I hugged Mom to calm her and also to avoid having to look at her since she was on the verge of tears. "I love you."

Dinner with my parents was surreal. I'd eaten with them for years just the three of us when Luke was at his mom's house, but it was the first time since leaving for college. I knew I wouldn't miss the crappy cafeteria food, but I missed the energy on campus. I felt like a stranger in my own house as Larry and my mom discussed work and other things that had happened without me knowing. Of course, I had a lot of things that had happened to me I wasn't about to discuss with them.

"Lydia," my stepdad said. "What's your favorite class so far?"

I set my fork down on my plate, stuffed from so much pot roast, and turned to Larry. "I'm not sure yet," I told him. "But Intro to Theatre is fun. I wish I could take more than one class in my major this first semester."

"Well, you have to get the basics for a degree," Larry said. "You'll get to take more theatre classes as you progress."

I zoned out as Larry reiterated the values of education. I knew he meant well, but I'd heard it a thousand times through high school even after I confirmed I wanted to go to college and not move to New York immediately to pursue acting. While Mom had always been concerned about my body and heart, Larry's concerns were for my mind.

Later in the evening, Phoebe came over to visit. I squealed when I saw her because her formerly long black hair was cropped short in an adorable pixie cut I could never pull off. "Oh my gosh! You didn't tell me you'd cut your hair," I said, touching the spiky ends. "You look amazing!"

"I've missed you!" she said, throwing her arms around me. "I feel like I haven't seen you in ages!"

We retreated to my room for our girl talk, giggling like we were still preteens talking about boys we crushed on. Things were going well with Phoebe's boyfriend as I figured. She and Sam were a good match, and I remembered how sweet they were together at our senior prom several months earlier.

Phoebe told me all about her heavy course load at the community college. At the rate she was going, she'd be able to transfer to a university as a junior by the time Sam finished his welding certification. Everything she said made a lot of sense and I envied the ease at which she discussed their future and plans to get a place together. I was fairly certain my parents would kill me if I even thought about living with a guy before marriage, but Phoebe's parents were a lot more liberal than mine.

It didn't take Phoebe long to beg for more info about Jason since I'd given her very few details over text.

"I need to see a pic of this guy," Phoebe gushed. "My standard searching skills turned up nothing for a long-haired Jason Caldwell."

I grabbed my phone to pull up his Instagram page, which wasn't under his name, but under "CaldJaswellington." Most of his photos were his artwork, but there were a couple of selfies of him near prints in the college art gallery.

"Okay, I see now," she said. "Those eyes are so blue I bet it feels like he can see through you, and he has a nice smile. And my gosh, what pretty hair. It sucks guys can have such pretty hair, doesn't it? He probably barely combs it, huh?"

"His hair is so soft, Phoebe, and you're right about the eyes. They're beautiful. I really like him."

"Do you like him because of who he is or because he's the first guy you've fooled around with?"

Her words hurt a bit, but she was only looking out for me. "Maybe he's the first guy I've fooled around with because he's the first one I've liked this much."

"Just making sure I don't need to plan a murder anytime soon. I don't want you to get hurt."

"I didn't question you this much when you started dating Sam."

Phoebe threw her hands up in the air. "That's because we've known him since kindergarten! I don't know Jason like that and neither do you."

She had a point. What she had with Sam had grown from friendship throughout their childhoods. It wasn't the same as the way I was getting to know Jason. Everything felt magical and dreamlike as we'd spent many hours talking. I couldn't imagine talking to anyone else for six hours straight and not getting bored. I wasn't sure if I could feel that way about a guy I'd known as a little boy.

"I'm kinda glad I haven't seen Jason pee his pants in front of the whole school at assembly."

"One time! When he was six and had a bladder infection!" Phoebe exclaimed. "Trust me, Sam's got his bladder and penis under control now and knows exactly what to do—."

"TMI! I don't want to know anything about Sam's penis!"

"What about Jason's? Got any action yet?"

I buried my face in my hands. "Maybe a little...but not the kind of action you're talking about."

"Oh? Is Lydia's virginity still standing?"

"For now, but probably not much longer. It'll be soon, I think. When I'm ready. I want to make sure we love each other, and it would be nice to be on the pill for a while first too."

I cringed as Phoebe gave me her version of the safe sex speech. I'd heard it all before, but never with such graphic detail. Coming from her and having grown up with the guy she was talking about made me feel queasy and I had to look away.

Phoebe reached out and grabbed my chin, turning me back to face her. "You better make him wear a condom, Lydia! I don't care how much he whines about it feeling better without one or it only being one time. Promise me."

"I will! I'm not stupid. I want to be extra careful to cover myself both ways. I can't travel around like I want to with a baby."

"Yeah, I can't see you as a young mom, but you also don't want any diseases to damage your health so you can't have a baby later."

Honestly, I was still on the fence about whether or not I wanted to be a mom at all. Being responsible for someone else's existence when I wanted a life of traveling around to act. It would be difficult to make it work, but it also wasn't anything I needed to decide at eighteen. I had years to consider all my life choices. One thing I did know was I didn't want to do life alone. I wanted someone by my side and Jason seemed to fit like no one else.

"I'm a little scared having sex will change everything with me and Jason," I admitted to Phoebe. "Like he'll expect it all the time and we won't talk as much anymore."

"If he does it right, you'll want it all the time too."

"Not the first time, though. It'll hurt, won't it?"

"It can be uncomfortable if you're not ready. You'll be okay as long as you don't overthink it or tense up too much."

We both jumped when something slammed into my bedroom door. I got up cautiously, worried my mom had been listening to us. I found our beagle, Roscoe, perched outside my door.

"You scared me, boy," I said, letting him in. He jumped up on my bed and exposed his belly.

"Your first time doesn't have to be painful," Phoebe continued as she rubbed Roscoe's belly, making him kick his leg and groan. "Make him go slow, use plenty of lube, and relax."

"I'll try to remember that," I said, scratching Roscoe behind the ear.

"Maybe Jason can come with you for Thanksgiving break, and Sam and I can double with you!"

"We'll see. It's still early to think about Thanksgiving. I'm not sure how he feels about meeting my family."

"If you're serious enough to have sex with him, he should be willing to meet your family. It can't be about only him. You're not a casual sex person. If he doesn't want something more, I don't think he's the right guy for you."

"I know."

I broke out my sketchbook to show Phoebe some of my still-life drawings from class and told her all about my new friends Vicki and Marienne and she told me about some of the people she'd met at college. She was glad to hear I was joining clubs and getting involved in my classes. Phoebe even promised she and Sam would try to come to the spring theatre production.

The plans gave me so much to look forward to in the upcoming new year, and I already felt like such a different person from high school. I felt older and more confident. I texted Jason, who said he was gaming with some friends. I told him I'd be back in town on Saturday if he wanted to hang out, and he said he'd talk to me then. I couldn't wait.

Chapter 13
June 12, 2024

When Wednesday morning rolls around, I get up, take a shower, and get dressed like I'm going to the workshop. Then I leave to go to the cemetery. Whenever I talk to my mom, Vicki, Phoebe, or Luke, I feel like I'm lying by not telling them about talking to Jason. Any of them would scold me for it, and I know I don't want to hear another lecture, especially today.

But I also recognize I need to see my therapist again because I want her help with the bad dreams I'm having about the night Jason almost died. Luckily, she has an opening late this afternoon, so I'll have plenty of time to drive back from the cemetery.

The drive is nice, although a bit cloudy. I don't even realize the time's passed until I arrive at the small grocery store near the cemetery where I stop to get some fresh flowers.

Later, I pull through the gates and park near a tree as mist starts to fall. I arrive at Marienne's graveside to find Jason already sitting on the bench.

"Good morning," he greets me.

"Hi."

"Have a good week?"

"It happened. I've been busy with my acting workshop and working."

"That's good. I'm glad you're staying busy."

"What have you been doing?" I place the bouquet next to Marienne's headstone and take a seat on the bench beside Jason.

"Not a lot. Thinking mainly."

"Yeah, I do a lot of that too."

"That doesn't surprise me."

"I dreamed about it again...about the night you almost died."

"I thought those dreams stopped a long time ago," he says, turning toward me. "You need to clear your mind before bed. Meditate or something."

I sigh. "I'm not telling you because I want advice or think you can help or anything."

"Stubborn as always."

"So why are you here every week? Are you getting anything out of these visits?"

"The question is, are *you* getting anything out of the visits?"

"Frustration."

"But yet you keep coming back."

"Maybe I'm not stubborn as much as I'm stupid. It's something we have in common I guess."

Jason chuckles. "I did some pretty dumbass things, didn't I?"

"You don't hold the monopoly on stupidity, but yeah, you did. I did too."

"Try to let it all go, and you'll sleep better."

"Again, not helpful."

The mist turns into drizzle as I stand to leave. Something about being caught in the rain with Jason grabs my heart like a vise and I can hardly breathe. I wish I could take his advice and let it all go, but it's not so easy. It's much easier to fall in love than it is to fall out of it.

My therapist's office smells the same as it did when I last went in April—a strange mixture of leftover pine scent and hot apple cider from the holidays. When I get called back to her office, I'm greeted with a new white sofa. I miss the old floral one.

Dr. Benson notices me staring at the sofa and urges me to give it a try. "It's not as comfortable as the old one," she says.

"But the old one took quite a bit of abuse throughout the years and finally collapsed."

"It's fine," I say, finally taking a seat. The sofa gives a little, but it doesn't envelop me in a hug like the old and familiar floral monstrosity.

"I was glad to hear you'd made another appointment, Lydia. Why don't you tell me what's been going on in your life since I last saw you?" Dr. Benson crosses her legs and adjusts her orange pants. I've never seen the woman wear a neutral, but I don't blame her. All the bright colors compliment her smooth brown skin.

I tell her all about work, my friends' happy relationships, and the workshop. Dr. Benson takes a few notes, but mostly she nods her head and listens. I notice her shaved hairdo has some new patches of grey in it and think it suits her.

"Okay, that's all good, but none of those things are why you're here. You can be truthful with me, Lydia. I felt like we were finally getting somewhere during your last visit before you shut down on me."

I swear she can see right through me. It's creepy and comforting at the same time. I take a deep breath and blurt out almost everything. "I started having bad dreams again. It's hard to go to sleep sometimes and I feel like there are some dark clouds following me around most of the time. I swear I'm taking the antidepressants, but I'm scared they're not enough sometimes."

Dr. Benson uncrosses her legs and leans forward. "The meds aren't meant to fix everything, Lydia. You still have a lot of work to do. I'm not sure if upping your dosage will help on its own. Now, how long's it been since you've seen your primary care doctor about the prescription?"

I glance down at my lap. "I think it was February, so I have to go back by the end of the summer to get my prescription refilled. He felt like every six months was a good call-back time for what I'm taking."

"Only if you're not having any problems," Dr. Benson says, taking notes on her clipboard. "I'd like you to call him for an appointment as soon as possible. It could be you need to switch medications or start something for your insomnia. We can work through more things in our sessions too."

"Okay." I feel relieved to have a plan. "I'm ready to feel better."

"Do you think your bad dreams and insomnia are triggered by something external?"

I nod. "It's been over a year now since the accident. I finally went to the cemetery and put flowers on Marienne's grave."

Dr. Benson puts down her pen. "And how did that make you feel?"

"Sad. Angry. Confused. Frustrated."

"It's normal to have conflicting emotions."

"What bothers me is as much as I miss Marienne, sometimes I miss Jason more. A lot of times, really. I still want to talk to him."

"What would you hope to accomplish if you could talk to him?"

"Closure, I guess. I still feel connected to him even though I don't want to be."

"And what would constitute closure for you?"

"Honestly, a heartfelt apology from him for hurting me so much. Since we can't exactly go back in time and erase it all."

"Nor can you go back in time and prevent the accident or its outcome. Do you remember what we talked about in previous sessions about what you can and can't control, Lydia?"

"I do, Dr. B. I know I can only control my own actions and reactions."

"I want you to think this next week of other ways you can get the closure you need on your own. Unfortunately, we can't always get the apologies we feel we deserve, and we have to move on anyway. It's not easy to let something or someone go."

I wipe away a stray tear that falls down my cheek. "I know."

"It was a year ago today that you attempted suicide. Are you having new thoughts of harming yourself, Lydia?"

I shake my head and bite my lip. "Not anymore. I know I'm capable of living, but the pain is suffocating me."

"What you need to say is this: I know I'm capable of living, *and* right now, the pain is suffocating me. It can get better tomorrow, next week, or next month. There's no correct timeframe for healing."

Dr. Benson hands me a tissue and I dry my face before repeating her words. I'm reminded of something she told me when we first met.

She said she didn't like to bullshit her patients. Healing hurts like hell, and it's the best investment anyone can make in themselves.

On Sunday, I take Larry to lunch for Father's Day and later plan to visit the cemetery near my parents' house where my dad and my grandparents are buried. Along the way, I stop at a dollar store to buy some flowers.

After dropping some colorful flowers into the vase between my mother's parents' graves, I walk across the cemetery to where my father and other grandparents rest. It's only been about four years since Grammy died, and I miss our conversations.

I kneel in front of my dad's headstone and place the red carnations near the base. "Happy Father's Day, Dad." I place my hand on the stone.

Anthony Wayne Dawson
1973–2006
Beloved Husband, Father, and Son

He was only thirty-three years old when he died, living only about a decade longer than my current age. He and Mom had been high school sweethearts married for thirteen years. On a normal summer day, he went to work like usual and never came home. He dropped to the floor during a marketing presentation and didn't regain consciousness. The autopsy revealed a ruptured aortic aneurysm. A freak bodily accident that could've happened to anyone, but it happened to my dad.

What could I accomplish if I only had ten years left to live? Would I still worry about finding romantic love or would I seek fulfillment in my career? How would my life have been different if Dad had lived? Would he and Mom still be together, and would I have any younger siblings? I wonder if Jason would have even been on my radar if my life were different. There's no guarantee I would have chosen the same college or even met Jason or Marienne. Maybe they'd still be alive.

But was the whole thing fate? My dad's untimely death, my mom's remarriage, meeting Marienne, falling in love with Jason only to lose him? Had Luke saved my life because death wasn't my destiny last year?

I reach out and run my fingers over the smooth stone, tracing the letters in my dad's name. I wish he could tell me what to do and if I'm on the right path. Though I've had dreams about my dad, I don't recall any of them in which he's spoken to me. Maybe someday he will, and I'll remember.

Chapter 14
October 5, 2019

Just when the secrecy of our relationship was making me worry about him hiding me from everyone, Jason invited me to go to a party on a Saturday night. A party meant other people would be there, so he couldn't have been hiding me if he wanted me there with him.

Jason picked me up a little after nine o'clock and told me the party was about a half-hour away from campus. I wasn't sure what to expect, but I didn't think it would be at a mobile home parked in a field in the middle of nowhere with absolutely no cell reception.

"Wow, your friend really does live out in the boonies," I said as I took in our surroundings. The mobile home was level enough on stacked cinder blocks, but the underpinning was busted in several places and the broken wooden steps at the front door looked like an invitation for tetanus.

There were a few older cars parked haphazardly around the overgrown yard and a pimped-up yellow sports car with black racing stripes parked under a portable carport. I could feel the bass of the music pumping in my chest as Jason and I got out of his truck.

"That's why we always have the parties at his house," Jason said. "There's no one around for miles to complain about the noise."

I checked my phone again for reception without luck. "And no phones either."

"Mack wanted to live off-the-grid, but he realized he was much more comfortable with electricity, water, and a landline."

"No kidding."

"I haven't drank much in a while, but I might drink tonight. We can stay until I sober up if you don't want to drive my truck to get us out of here unless you're planning to drink too."

"I'm underage." I immediately felt like a loser when Jason smirked at me.

"There's no cops here."

Just then, a short guy with long greasy black hair and a lumberjack beard stumbled out the front door, laughing as he fell off the bottom step and landed on the ground. "Jason, man!" he yelled. "You made it!"

"Yeah, man," Jason said, reaching his hand down to help the guy up. "Lydia, Mack. Mack, Lydia."

"Hi," I said. "Are you hurt?"

"I'm good," he said. "I keep meaning to fix that goddamn step so my ex-bitch'll let my son come to visit."

I followed Jason and Mack up the unstable stairs and into the living room. Inside, the place was smoky and had a skunk-like aroma. There were crushed beer cans, full cans, and assorted bottles of clear and brown liquor stacked on a card table with one shorter leg held up with a stack of old phone books. A bong sat in the middle in place of any flower arrangement décor I'd expect to find on a table. I knew then I'd made a mistake in going to the party. It was nothing like theatre parties I'd attended. I glanced around at the four other people in the room and wiped my palms on my jeans.

Jason plopped down on a threadbare brown sofa beside a woman with a half-shaved head and dark red eyeliner. I sat on his other side close to the couch's arm where it looked like the fabric had melted.

"Everyone, this is Lydia. Lydia, this is everyone."

I swallowed hard as the people around the room told me their names. The shaved-head woman was Lila, who introduced herself as Mack's "new bitch" and didn't say another word the entire evening. The guy with curly red hair and an eyebrow ring who was sprawled out in the corner was Will.

There was a stringy-haired blonde woman named Kay in the armchair channeling the "heroin chic" look. Kay was there with her sister, Bobbie, who looked like a girl scout dressed in a brown sheath dress the color of a UPS uniform. Her brown hair was pulled into a high ponytail. She looked young and sweet except for the spiked dog collar she wore as a necklace—there was nothing innocent about that.

After an incredibly long silence while the crew stared at me, Mack asked if I wanted something to drink, and I declined, uneasy about my surroundings. I felt a little better when Jason grabbed a bottle of water for me and started chatting with Will about classes.

"Yeah," Will said. "One more semester and I'll start applying to med schools. I don't care where I go since nothing's holding me down here."

"Gee, thanks," Kay barked.

"You can come with me, baby," Will said, and then Kay got up and straddled him, giving him a big sloppy kiss that seemed to be the start of something.

"I haven't decided yet on grad school," Jason said, ignoring the couple dry humping in the corner. "I'll figure it out when I get back from Europe. What's up with you, Bobbie?"

Wait. Europe? He hadn't mentioned going to Europe soon. I would have to ask about it later.

Bobbie shrugged. "Babysitting Kay, as usual," she said in perfect monotone. "She can't seem to keep a job or get her head out of Will's ass long enough to take any classes."

Jason chuckled, and I wondered how he knew these people. Had he gone to school with any of them? He must have read my mind because he answered me. "Bobbie, Will, and me graduated together, and Mack's a football legend from two years before us."

"Oh," I said. "And what's this about a trip to Europe?"

Before Jason could answer, the already loud music became deafening and Mack squealed along with it, playing air drums. Then he turned down the volume to its previous roar and yelled, "Top of the hour's coming! Time for minute shots, bitches!"

I looked at my phone to see the time. It was only almost ten o'clock and I already felt like I'd been trapped in the uncomfortable shithole for hours instead of minutes.

Everyone went into the adjacent kitchen, which was decorated with overflowing trashcans and smelled like the inside of a deep fryer. Jason joined the others around a beat-up farmhouse table with two benches and mismatched chairs on the ends. Not knowing what to do, I perched on the only bar stool in the corner and prepared myself for watching the event. I sure as hell didn't want to participate considering I had no idea what the game entailed.

Apparently, "minute shots" were just that. Shot glasses of beer drank at the beginning of each minute for one hour. I tried to figure out how much alcohol it would be, but my brain tapped out. Hundreds of reasons swirled in my head about why it was a bad idea, but before I could articulate my thoughts, the game had already started.

Jason and I were the only ones not participating, and while I could withstand the pressure of Jason's friends egging me on to join them, he couldn't.

At fifteen minutes past ten, Jason downed the last half of a large bottle of some kind of brown liquor in an agreement to catch up with the others. Then, he joined in on the shots. It all happened fast, and I was afraid to embarrass him by protesting.

I'd been around buzzed people before, but I'd never seen a group drinking shots so quickly. What started out as giggling and hollering soon became glassy-eyed laughter and slurred words. I had no idea what the alcohol content of beer was or how much it would take to get someone drunk. I didn't know what the others had drunk before we arrived and worried about what was in the bottle Jason had finished. I looked around from my spot on the stool to find the bottle, but it was already tossed away somewhere out of sight.

All I could do was watch in fascination and horror as the guy I'd walked in with turned into someone else before my eyes—a headbanging, air-drumming, shot-drinking, loudmouth who didn't seem to care if I was there or not.

By the end of the hour, Kay had her head on the table and Bobbie was giggling constantly. Lila still looked stone-cold sober, and Mack was mellower than before. Jason had tied his hair in a knot on top of his head, and Will was staring at me so intensely I had to look away, pulling out my phone to check the time again.

"I hope you don't have a weak stomach," Will said.

When no one answered, I realized he was talking to me. "What?"

He dragged an outdoor-sized trashcan over to the side of the table and then looked at me again. "You might wanna look away if you do."

I should have turned away faster because Will proceeded to stick two fingers down his throat to gag himself until he had spewed all the contents of his stomach loudly and disgustingly into the can.

"You're such a wimp," Bobbie said, turning away. "Whoever pukes first is out."

"Whatever," Will said, coughing and wiping tears from his eyes as he shoved the trashcan away. "I'm not gonna let that shit metabolize and screw my liver."

I guess he had no problem with potential damage to his stomach, esophagus, and teeth. And this guy wanted to be a doctor? I was too stunned to comment.

"Fuck," Jason muttered, slamming his head on the table. "That shit stinks. Get the can outta here before I blow chunks, you fuckin' pussy."

I had to get out of there too. It's not that I'd never heard a word I loathed spoken before, but I certainly didn't want to hear it from the mouth of the guy I was dating. I stood up and ran to the front door, slamming it behind me.

The only light outside came from the moon and the pathetic glow of the yellow bulb in the fixture by the door. I stumbled down the steps and made my way to Jason's truck, so mad I could cry. Finding it locked—seriously, like anyone would steal it out there—I cursed and slammed my hand against the window. Not wanting to go back inside, I pulled open the tailgate and sat on the end of it, leaning down to catch my breath.

A few minutes later, the door swung open and bounced against the side of the mobile home. Mack stuck his head out. He went back inside and then came out again, leading Jason down the stairs. Once they were steady on their feet, Mack walked Jason over to the tailgate and sat him down beside me before stomping back to the rickety steps, carefully managing to get inside, and slamming the door behind him.

I sighed as I looked at the mess of a man beside me. He reeked of alcohol and now had his hair hanging around his face. I brushed his hair back with my fingers and put it in a ponytail with the rubber band he had on his wrist.

"Thanks," he said. "Why you out by yourself?"

"Well, technically, I'm out here with you. I had to get away from you and all your drunk-ass friends acting like fools in there."

"We just having...some fun."

"That's fun for you? Watching someone puke up beer and God knows what else?"

"Well, that...wasn't..."

I shivered and rubbed my arms.

"Cold?"

"I'm fine," I snapped.

Jason shrugged off his jacket and tried to wrap it around my shoulders. I took it out of his hands and put it on, thankful it didn't stink too badly.

"It's one thing to have a drink or two, but what you did in there was reckless, Jason. What did you drink before the beer? How much alcohol was in that stuff?"

"Re-ax," he slurred.

"Don't tell me to fucking relax!"

"You sexy...you say 'fuck.'"

"Oh my God! Just shut up. You're completely wasted and don't know what you're saying anyway."

He stood up and steadied himself against the back of the truck. "I gotta piss," he said. "Be back."

I watched Jason as he stepped to the side of the trailer and had to turn away as he dropped his pants and underwear to his ankles like a little boy learning to pee outside. Eventually, after he seemed to have emptied his bladder of liquids he hadn't even drunk yet, he stumbled back in my direction. Instead of sitting down with me, he kept walking to the other side of the yard where he half fell, half collapsed onto the ground.

"Jason!" I bailed off the tailgate and ran over to him, squatting beside him in the grass. "Are you okay?"

"Fine," he mumbled, attempting to sit up. He failed and knocked me off balance onto my ass. Once I'd stretched my legs out in front of myself, Jason put his head in my lap. "Give me...minute...sober up...take you...home."

"No. You're not driving anywhere." I reached into his pocket and took his keys.

"Mmm kay," he said, snuggling into my lap. "You take truck."

"I'm good where I am. Just rest for a while."

In his drunken state, I doubted Jason remembered there was no cell service and I had no idea where the hell we were to even think about trying to drive my way out in an unfamiliar vehicle. And besides—even as pissed as I was—did he actually expect me to leave him lying in a yard in the middle of nowhere?

"You okay?" I asked again.

"Mmm hmm," he mumbled. "Comfortable now."

"That makes one of us," I muttered, shifting to move a small rock from underneath me.

"I could talk to...all night...you stand...you *under*stand." I kept quiet and caressed his forehead. The moon gave enough light for me to see his eyes were still closed. I wasn't sure if he knew who I was. "Never met...anyone...you before. We supposed to...to meet. I know...you know...me, Lydia...don't leave...me."

"I'm here." I reached for his hand and held it over his chest.

"I want...die...years ago before I...I figured...too scared...do it. I had rope...I couldn't. I...thinking... parents find me...barn. I...keep going."

The liquor was like a jumbled-up truth serum. "I don't know what to say other than I'm glad you didn't go through with it. Did you get help?"

"There's no help...disaster."

"It doesn't have to be that way."

"I'm figging shit out. I go...get out...this town."

"We're all figuring out shit. Will you come back?"

"Maybe. I don't know...what I wanna do. There's nothing...keeping me...right now."

His words stung. Was I nothing? "That's why you don't want a girlfriend."

"I need...answer to...myself now."

"Then why even bother dating?" I asked, tears pooling in my eyes.

"I'm drawn...to you, but if...care too much...push...you away."

"That doesn't make sense."

"I think...time together gonna...it be short." Jason curled up on his side with his head facing my stomach and started snoring through his open mouth.

I sighed and leaned back on my hands, unsure what to make of his ramblings. Why would he push me away if he cared too much? It didn't make any sense.

Later, after getting lost in my thoughts while listening to the sounds of nature around me, a quick glance at my phone told me it was close to midnight. I placed it on the dirt beside me. The bass from the music inside seemed to vibrate through my chest right before it shut off.

I looked at the trailer windows. The kitchen light was out and only a soft glow remained through the living room window and the tiny vertical window in the front door.

Jason rolled to his back and then coughed like he was struggling to breathe, startling me.

"Jason!" I grabbed my phone and shined the flashlight in his face. His eyes fluttered a bit and then rolled back in his head. His lips looked blue. I shook him, but he didn't stir. "Jason! Wake up." I pushed him off my lap and kneeled above him.

Slapping the sides of his face didn't help. I shook him more violently and then leaned down to see if I could hear his breath. I couldn't. I pressed his neck for a pulse, but I couldn't feel anything except my own heart pounding, its pulsing drowning out every other sound around me. A cold sweat prickled all over my body.

I screamed and pounded on Jason's chest. Suddenly, all my years-old CPR training resurfaced, and I remembered to tilt Jason's head back to give him two puffs of air before starting chest compressions. I screamed again for help after giving him more air, praying for someone inside to be sober enough to hear me and come outside. Time seemed to have stopped while I was pressing on Jason's chest, but then someone pushed me to the side and took over the compressions, keeping up my count. It was Will.

"How long's he been down?" Will asked, still pumping Jason's chest. "Give him breaths!"

I gave Jason two breaths. "Not long!"

Someone else walked up beside us, and I didn't bother looking up to see who it was. Will yelled at them. "Call nine-one-one! He's not breathing!" The person took off running.

Will kept doing chest compressions. I couldn't stop shaking, but I kept breathing for Jason until his eyes started fluttering and he started choking. "Jason! Oh my God!"

We rolled Jason to his side as he started vomiting. I didn't care that he was getting it all over me and Will didn't seem to mind either. I'd never been so relieved in my life, and I started sobbing as I held Jason, pressing my hand against his chest to feel his heart beating.

Early morning was a blur from the paramedics arriving and transporting Jason to the hospital. I had jumped into the back of the ambulance after he was loaded to ride along. On the way, I answered as many questions as I could, not letting go of Jason's hand.

In the emergency room, I was left in a waiting room where I sat trembling, having removed Jason's puke-splattered jacket. I didn't have Jason's phone and had no idea how to get ahold of his parents. I took a couple of deep breaths to calm myself before calling Marienne.

As soon as Marienne picked up, I started crying again.

"Lydia, what's wrong?" she mumbled, stifling a yawn.

"It's Jason," I said.

"Do I need to kill my cousin? What'd the asshole do?"

"No. Not that. I need you to call his parents. We're at the hospital."

"Whoa...what?" She sounded wide awake.

I gave her a quick version of what had happened, and she promised to let her parents and her aunt and uncle know. When I'd thought about wanting to meet their family before, I had wanted better circumstances.

Jason's parents and Marienne's parents seemed like two average fifty-something couples during our brief exchange, but I didn't have the capacity to meet them any more than they could give the energy to truly introduce themselves given the circumstances. Both men were tall with grey hair and similar features showing their relation as brothers. Jason's mother was petite with long dark hair, and Marienne's mom was supermodel tall with a stylish platinum-hued short haircut.

I found myself retelling the night's events for a third time, but this time getting hammered with questions from Jason's parents.

"So, you don't know what kind of liquor he drank before all the beer?" his mom asked.

"No," I said, tears filling my eyes again. "I'm not a drinker. I know it was a big bottle and the liquid was brown. He downed it so fast after changing his mind about playing the game. I didn't have time to try to stop him."

"Of course not," she said.

"He's always been susceptible to peer pressure," Jason's dad said, looking at me and then his wife. "It could have been bourbon or diesel and Jason would've drunk it if his friends were egging him on."

"No, that's not what I mean," Jason's mom said, taking my hand. "I'm not implying Lydia was responsible for him. If anything, he should have been looking out for her. I'm only trying to figure out what it might have been."

"I'm sorry I couldn't stop him," I told them. "I didn't know what kind of party it was going to be, and I was the only one there who wasn't drinking."

Marienne's mom had walked across the room to get coffee for her sister-in-law, and she sat down next to me as she handed over the cup. "From what it sounds like, being probably the youngest person there didn't make you the least mature," she said. "How old are you, Lydia? Eighteen? Nineteen?"

"I'm eighteen."

"Well, at twenty-two, I'd hoped our son had come to his senses about not drinking like that, but I guess we were wrong," Jason's dad said.

His mom nodded and wiped her eyes. "I'm sorry you had to go through that, Lydia."

"I'm fine," I said. "I just want Jason to be okay."

"We all want that," Marienne's mom said.

Chapter 15
June 17, 2024

I find myself looking forward to hanging out with Kolton and some of the others from the workshop during our lunch break. Nel and Tom are partnered for class, as well as Tanya and Jake. We've gotten close with the acting exercises. Of course, Kolton and I have grown the closest with all the inside jokes we've shared as partners.

The six of us pile into a booth at the diner near the auditorium and immediately start talking about the upcoming exercise.

"Does Bernetta expect us to share a real secret on stage?" Tanya twirls a loose braid around her fingertips. She has her hair fixed in an elaborate high bun today and it looks amazing on her.

Quite the opposite with his hair, having hardly any, Jake runs his hand across his head before shrugging his shoulders. "How would she even know the difference?"

Tom shakes his head. "I don't know that I have any secrets worth sharing, so I'll probably make something up as it is."

"She probably has lie-detector radar or something," Nel says. "I don't know if I'd risk lying to her."

"Acting's lying anyway," argues Jake. "We can all handle it."

Kolton grins at me from across the table. "Depends on your acting method I suppose," he says. "You planning to share a deep, dark secret, Lydia?"

"I guess I could tell everyone about all the episodes of *Little House on the Prairie* I've streamed during the last year. That's a pretty dark secret."

Jake almost does a spit-take. "I thought I was the only person who still watched those," he says after recovering from being strangled on his water. "I feel seen now, Lydia."

We all burst into laughter. I have another secret in mind I'm finally ready to talk about with people I don't think will judge me, but I don't want to say anything until we're back in class. It will be better when everyone's in a semicircle on stage so I can see reactions.

Back in class, we draw numbers and Kolton's in the spotlight first to share a secret. He leans forward in the metal folding chair and clasps his hands together. "About a year ago, I found out my girlfriend of almost a year had been cheating on me with my best friend," he begins. "It hurt that both of them would betray me like that, as well as a few friends who knew what was going on and never told me. I pretty much dropped them all and found some better friends, but I still think about my ex and my ex-best friend.

"When I found out they were living together shortly after everything went to shit, I did something petty. I can't say I'm ashamed of it necessarily, but it might have caused some problems in their relationship. I requested some lingerie catalogs in my former friend's name and had them sent to their address. That was one thing my ex always hated—those types of catalogs— because she said they objectified women with advertising so clearly aimed at heterosexual men."

While I don't find Kolton's revelation too shocking, I wonder what others in our class might share and whether or not their secrets will be true or fabricated.

Jake's up next, but he remains standing behind the chair, bracing his hands on the back. "So, when I was a little kid—like ten—my grandma gave me this antique watch that belonged to my granddad. I kept it for a few years because it meant so much to me. Granddad was the only father figure I had, so I really loved him and was lost when he died.

"Anyway, when I was using, I pawned it to get some quick cash and told my grandma it was stolen. She died last year, and I never told her the truth about the watch. She was always supportive of me and so proud I stayed clean after jail. If there's life after death, I hope both of 'em know how shitty I feel about doing that." He bows his head and takes a deep breath before returning to his seat.

When Nel stands to take her turn, I notice she's fixed her hair since lunch and it's now hanging in two braids over her shoulders. It reminds me of Jason's hair the first time we met, and I have to focus hard on Nel's story to keep from drowning in my memories.

"I told you all about my daughter in another class," Nel says, taking a seat and crossing her long legs at the ankles. "The adoption is semi-open, meaning I get updates and photos of her once a year sent through the attorney's office and she'll be able to contact me when she's eighteen. I'm not supposed to make any contact with her or her parents directly to protect their privacy.

"Well, one of my friends worked as an intern over the summer in the office and gave me the address for where my daughter lives. I would never do anything to hurt her or try to take her or anything, but I drove by her house to see it once. It's beautiful, and I caught a glimpse of her playing through the front window with her dad. It made me feel good to know she's safe and loved."

My place is fourth in line, and my stomach is churning as I stand to share my secret. I sit in the chair and look around the stage at my classmates. Kolton gives me an encouraging wink and I wipe my sweaty hands on my jeans before beginning.

"Last summer after my friend died, I was in a really bad place mentally," I tell them. "I'm doing a lot better now, but I had to stay in the hospital psychiatric ward for two weeks after I tried to kill myself."

Kolton's expression changes, and I worry I've shared too much, but I have to keep going.

"I take antidepressants now along with going to therapy to keep those dark thoughts away. I don't ever want to get back to that place again since I've learned living with pain can still feel like being alive sometimes."

I leave center stage to take my seat and as I do, Kolton stands, followed by Jake and Nel. Soon everyone else in class is standing too. Kolton steps forward and gives me a hug and then my classmates do the same, one at a time. By the end of the receiving line of hugs, my heart feels full. These are my people.

Of course, I don't expect Bernetta to announce kissing practice next. With our partners, we have to share one simple peck and then one passionate kiss in front of the group. A few of the plays I'd done during college had kissing roles for me, but I hadn't done a stage kiss since junior year. I haven't really kissed anyone but Jason since he and I started dating, even after things had fizzled out with us. The thought of someone else's lips touching mine after more than a year makes my whole face tingle.

The simple peck with Kolton goes perfectly. He's gentle and polite. Then, we mutually agree to stage our passionate kiss during a fight scene, and it plays off beautifully with Kolton running after me to apologize for forgetting our anniversary. He grabs my hand and spins me around, pulling me close to him. As I look up, he wipes away my tears with his thumbs and then kisses me so hard I can feel it in my toes. I have to wrap my arms around his neck to keep from tumbling backward.

In the brief moment after Bernetta yells "Cut!" I can't look away from Kolton's eyes as he stares into mine. I let my eyes drop and watch his nostrils flare as he lets out a breath. His Adam's apple bobs in his throat as he swallows and takes another deep breath. I hope no one can see I'm shaking as I return to my chair to watch the next couple.

After the workshop, Kolton walks me to my car and lingers there as I unlock it. I drop my bag inside and turn to face him. He gives me a half-smile and holds onto the top of my door.

"Just say it," I tell him.

"Say what?"

"Whatever it is you have to say. After what I shared in there, I understand if you want to distance yourself from the crazy woman." I look down at my shoes, realizing how dirty they are.

"Lydia..." He moves my chin and makes me look at him. "Why would I want to distance myself from you? I'd like to think we're well on our way to becoming friends—good friends. I'm sad you felt so much pain in the past that it overwhelmed you, but I'm also glad you've overcome it to get better."

Better. The word flashes in front of me like a neon marquee. *Was I better?*

"It took a lot of courage for you to share your story with everyone," he continues. "I'd say yours was the most personal. A lot more revealing than my dirty catalog prank."

I take a cleansing breath, determined to be more open than I have in the past. "What if I'm not better, Kolton? Does it change how you feel about our friendship?"

"What do you mean?"

"I'm still struggling. I don't know if I'll ever be 'better' now or in the future."

"We're all struggling works-in-progress. I didn't even reveal the worst thing I did. I also sent gay porn email subscriptions to the church group that ousted my sister. Every single one of them who had addresses listed in the directory. I shouldn't still be holding on to all the anger so many years later."

"I'm still seeing my shrink and taking meds just to function. I live in my parents' house, and it still feels like they're watching me—especially with the anniversary of my attempt just a few days ago. Not that we'll acknowledge it. It's not exactly something worth celebrating. And when I talk to my two closest friends...they still look at me with pity. I'm a mess."

"Our kiss wasn't a mess," he says, dropping his hand to my shoulder.

"It was acting, Kolton. It's the one thing I've always been good at—acting like I was okay when I wasn't...until I just couldn't fake it anymore."

"The first kiss might have been acting, but the second one felt like something more. At least, it did to me."

My cheeks start burning, and I know he's right.

Kolton puts his hands in his pockets and rocks back on his heels. "What I'm saying is I *wanted* to kiss you. I've wanted to since we started talking, and I'd like to do it again sometime, preferably without an audience. Like after a date. Take that info and do with it what you will—no pressure. See ya."

He walks to his car, leaving me behind.

"I don't know what to do with it," I say to myself as I drop into my seat. My eyes sting as I start the car and I have to sit for a few minutes to let the air conditioner dry my cheeks.

I bring artificial gerbera daisies with me when I stop by Marienne's grave later that week since they'll last longer than real flowers. I pick off the dried remains of last week's flowers and walk them to the decorative trash can at the end of the row of graves.

When I turn around, Jason is walking toward me. I look down at my feet and take a deep breath before heading back to the bench near Marienne's resting place. I know I shouldn't, but I feel so guilty about the kiss with Kolton yesterday. I know it shows all over my face.

"We meet again," Jason says as I sit beside him.

"I come here at the same time each week, so it's not that surprising you'd find me here."

"Maybe it's me who comes here at the same time each week and you're finding me."

"Does it matter?"

"I don't know. Does it matter to you?"

"Yes!" I throw my hands up in the air. "Has anyone or anything ever mattered to you, Jason?"

"I'm sensing some hostility here, and I don't know how to answer your question."

"Let's simplify it. Do I matter to you? Did I ever?"

Jason looks down at Marienne's headstone. "How can you ask me that?"

"It's easy. I open my mouth and speak what's on my mind. I've been working hard this past year trying to love myself and sometimes it means asking difficult questions. Questions I'm not even sure I want answers to."

"You deserve to be happy, Lydia."

"Don't you think I know that? But despite it all, I almost killed myself last year, Jason! I've been in therapy ever since trying to make sense of the mess inside my head. I'm trying to make new friends and not feel pain every single waking moment."

"It's my fault?"

"Things you did contributed," I say. "But no, it's my fault for letting you hurt me so much. I should have known better, and I should've listened to my friends when they told me I deserved better."

"How'd you do it, Lydia? What'd you do to yourself?"

"Pills. Sleeping pills, pain pills...everything I could get my hands on. I thought I could just go to sleep and not wake up, but my stepbrother came home on a whim and saved my life. If he'd gotten there an hour later, I probably would've died."

Jason looks at me with a blank expression.

"I don't even know why I'm telling you this...or maybe I do. You're probably the only person who doesn't care enough to judge me or be concerned about it."

"Do you really think that's true?"

I stand up to leave. "I'm not sure I know what's true anymore."

Jason stands and reaches out for me, but I step back. "Of course, I cared about you."

"Well, you had a real shitty way of showing it."

Chapter 16
October 6, 2019

I waited with Marienne and her family until a doctor came out and spoke to them. Staying behind Marienne and her parents, I overheard the phrases "alcohol poisoning" and "lucky to be alive" before the doctor offered to take the Caldwells back to see him.

Marienne had insisted on taking me back to the dorm with her after Jason's parents went to his room. I didn't want to leave him, but I had no ride otherwise. It was late Sunday morning when we pulled into the parking lot on campus. Marienne shut off the engine but didn't make a move to get out.

"Talk to me," she said.

I turned to face her and shook my head.

"I want to tell you I'm surprised by what happened last night with Jason, but I can't. He's done some pretty stupid shit involving alcohol; it just hasn't gotten as bad. On his twenty-first birthday, one of his dumbass friends dropped him off in my front yard instead of his own. They left him there in the middle of the night. My dad found him the next morning covered in his own piss and puke. Dad turned the hose on Jason to get him up."

I didn't have a response.

"We hoped he'd learned his lesson, but it happened a couple of times before my dad and my uncle said something. Jason straightened up for a while, but I guess the stint of better behavior is over. I don't know what my aunt and uncle might do now. Threaten rehab or kick him out of their house. Stop paying his tuition if he doesn't become more responsible."

"I was disgusted with how he acted at the party around his friends. He became a stranger for a while, but then when we were alone, he was opening up to me before..."

Marienne took my hand in hers. "I don't have to tell you how serious this is. Jason would have died tonight if you weren't there. I'm grateful to you because as screwed up as he is, I love my cousin. The best thing you can do to save yourself a lot of heartache is to take a step back from seeing him. Because I love you too."

The main problem was I was fairly sure I loved Jason too, especially after seeing him in such a vulnerable state. "I shouldn't walk away from him because he made a mistake. I don't think I can."

"The thing is, though, you can't exist for him just to save him from himself. He has to want to get better, and I hope to God he does after this. But it's not something that should be your problem, Lydia. No matter how much you care about him—even if you are his girlfriend or whatever you two are calling your relationship."

"I don't know what to do. But I know I care about him."

"I don't think it's possible for you to *not* care about someone."

I didn't hear from Jason all week, and I was a nervous wreck because of it. Marienne assured me he was fine, but I was still worried. Jason taking a week off from classes wasn't unexpected considering what he'd been through, but I'd hoped he would call or text me.

Contacting him first seemed out of the question, mainly due to the fear of not knowing what to say. What did you say to someone who'd almost died? And what did I do with the feeling of dread in my gut that came from realizing I loved him at the same time I felt I was losing him?

In all my worrying about Jason, I'd also failed to check in with my mother during the week. By Friday, she'd left me two messages to call her, so I finally did after my last class for the week.

"I thought I was going to have to drive there to get you to talk to me," she said as her way of answering the phone.

"Sorry, Mom. What's up?"

"Call it 'mother's intuition' if you like, but I was worried there was something wrong. Is everything okay?"

"I've been super busy with classes this week," I lied. "Nothing's wrong."

"Okay. Well, are you coming home this weekend?"

There was no way I could keep up the "okay" charade if I had to face her. "I can't this weekend. I have a lot of work to do in the library, so I won't fall behind in my classes. Maybe next weekend."

"I might have to work that Saturday," Mom sighed.

"Well, then the weekend after that. I'll come visit soon. I promise."

After ending the call, I threw myself onto my bed and pulled the pillow over my head. It was only two in the afternoon, but I was exhausted and needed a nap before Marienne returned from her classes. While I had filled my mornings with gen ed requirements, she'd opted for mostly afternoon classes for hers.

A couple of hours later, Marienne was back to pack her overnight bag. She'd been going home every weekend to be closer to her part-time job. Vicki had also gone home a lot since she missed her boyfriend.

"Sure you don't want to go to my parents' house with me?" she asked while shoving the last of her laundry into her collapsible hamper. "I know they won't mind."

"I don't want to go anywhere," I said. "I'd rather stay in and watch YouTube videos all night."

"Okay, but if you change your mind, come on out. I'll text you the address. It's super easy to find with GPS."

"I appreciate it."

Of course, once she left, I went back to sleep, not even bothering to set an alarm to eat dinner in the cafeteria. I had plenty of snacks in the room, not that I felt much like eating them with the thoughts scrambled in my head and trickling down into my stomach.

I woke up suddenly and realized it was dark outside. I wasn't sure what had startled me out of my sleep until I heard knocking on my window. I hopped off the bed and walked over without bothering to turn on the lights. I pulled up the blinds and found Jason standing there with his hands in his pockets. From the tennis court lights shining behind him, I could see his hair was down and had been cut to a length just brushing his shoulders.

"Wanna go for a walk?" he asked as soon as I opened the window.

"Sure," I said. "I'll grab my phone and ID and meet you at the front door." Then I closed the window without giving him a chance to argue. I didn't want to climb through the window and leave it unlocked while I was gone. Plus, I needed an extra minute to slip on my shoes and take a few deep breaths before seeing him again.

"I missed you at the Art Club meeting," I told him as we walked past the Art Building. "It wasn't the same with Nora running the show."

"She'll run it soon enough when I'm done with classes."

"I guess so. Will you graduate in December or May?"

"I'm supposed to graduate in May or possibly December of next year depending on how well my classes go in my study-abroad program that starts next semester. Finally, according to my parents. Although taking five years to get a bachelor's degree isn't too crazy."

Study-abroad program? I thought he'd only been talking about a trip to Europe during his drunken stupor. "I didn't realize you weren't staying here to finish your degree."

"I guess it didn't come up. It's a year-long program."

"But it should have. It's something you should share with someone you're dating."

He shrugged and sat down on a bench in between two buildings. It was well-lit but still secluded enough to offer some privacy. I sat down close beside him and then he slid away and turned to face me. I looked at him and wondered if I should speak or wait to let him start talking again.

Finally, I couldn't take it anymore. "What happened last week really scared me, Jason."

He pulled his now shorter hair into a low ponytail and took a deep breath. "I'll admit it wasn't my finest moment."

"You could have died."

"But I didn't."

"Do you remember anything about the party? About what all you did?"

Jason shook his head. "I remember waking up in the hospital with my mom crying and my dad pissed at me. They said they'd met my girlfriend and that she'd saved my life. I was pretty confused, and then I remembered a bit about going to the party.

"Mari chewed me out pretty good too, despite not being at the party. She called me irresponsible and a bunch of other insults that ran together."

"You made a mistake, Jason, but it doesn't make you a bad person. It could have just as easily been someone else at the party."

"Well, anyone but you, since you weren't drinking, right?"

"What does my not drinking have to do with any of this?"

"Nothing, I guess. Look, I talked to Will, and he told me you and him did CPR before the ambulance came. I never know if he's full of shit..."

"It's true." My stomach rolled as I recalled that night. "You were sleeping on me and all of sudden you started choking. The next thing I knew, you turned blue and had stopped breathing. I couldn't find a pulse either, so I started CPR and screamed for help. Will's the one who came outside and started helping with the chest compressions."

"I guess I have him to thank for the fractured rib."

"Probably. It all happened so fast. We worked hard to get you breathing again."

"So, we were outside?"

"Uh-huh. I went out there to get some air and Mark brought you outside. We never went back in." I bit my lip to keep my tears at bay.

"You mean Mack?"

"Whatever. It's not like we're gonna follow each other on Instagram."

"He's been my friend for a long time."

"Yes, I know. You told me. Was his party seriously your idea of fun?"

"You need to lighten up sometimes, Lydia. Don't you ever want to do that?"

"Jason, having a drink or two is fine, but you almost dying in my arms wasn't what I consider fun or lightening up."

"I didn't mean to ruin your evening," he said, looking down at his hands. "I usually hold my liquor better."

"That's not what Marienne said."

"My cousin doesn't know what she's talking about."

"Maybe you don't."

"I don't need you and Mari ganging up on me."

"What do you need then? I haven't heard from you all week, and then you show up at my dorm without calling or texting first and want to go on a walk."

"I just wanted to talk to you, I guess. Say thanks for what you did."

"You're welcome." It was on the tip of my tongue to tell him about the rest of the night and what I'd realized about how I felt about him, but it wasn't the right time.

"I think it's time for you to see other people."

"What?" I wasn't one hundred percent sure I'd heard him right as the racing of my pulse was making me dizzy. "What do you mean?"

"I think seeing other people's a good idea since I'll be studying abroad next year. It's only a few months away. I don't want you to get too attached to me."

My stomach burned although I hadn't eaten since lunch. "I don't want to," I blurted. "I just want to see you." *This can't be happening*, I thought. *I love him.*

"There's lots of people out there," he said, leaning his head down and covering his eyes with his hand.

"But I don't want other people, Jason. I want you. I—I love you."

His head popped up and his eyes took on the terror of a wild animal caught in a car's headlights. "You don't know me well enough to love me and if you knew me well you definitely wouldn't be saying it."

I could no longer hold back my tears. "Don't tell me how to feel. I know how I feel about you, you asshole. I might have realized it when you went to the hospital, but it doesn't mean it's not real."

"Don't cry," Jason said, putting his arm around me. "You're only infatuated with me, Lydia. It'll pass."

I pushed his arm off me and got up to walk away but he followed close behind.

"Wait, slow down," he said.

"I should have never gone out with you in the first place," I said, still trying to out-walk him. "This always happens to me. I'm not fun enough, or not pretty enough, or not girlfriend material. Or hell, maybe I'm all three!"

Jason grabbed my arm and spun me around to face him. "Stop. None of that's true."

"Leave me alone!" I tried to push him away, and he winced as I touched his chest. "I'm sorry...your ribs." I'd forgotten about the fracture.

But Jason didn't leave me alone. He pulled me closer and kissed my tear-stained cheek before finding my lips. I wrapped myself around him to kiss him back, and then he pulled away a bit. "You are beautiful, Lydia," he said. "And you are girlfriend material. I just think there's someone else out there for you, someone better for you who can stay here and be with you right now. Someone who isn't me."

"You don't know everything."

"Look, I'm not saying we can't see each other or be friends," he said after hugging me for a bit longer while I cried. "Think about what I said. It would be hard to do this long distance."

"Fine," I said. "I'm going back to my dorm."

I left Jason standing in the center of campus and sprinted back to the building. I barely made it inside the room before I dropped to the floor and sobbed. It wasn't exactly a breakup since we weren't officially together, but it sure felt like one.

Chapter 17
June 19, 2024

"So, I've been thinking a lot about the dreams I've been having about when Jason almost died," I blurt out to Dr. Benson before she can settle into her chair across from me. We've planned weekly sessions to help with my current issues. "It's always the same as it happened in real life, only the ending's bad. He always dies because I'm unable to save him. I think part of me, a really bad part of me wishes he had died then to get the heartache out of the way earlier. I feel so terrible even saying it out loud."

"You shouldn't feel terrible admitting how you're feeling," she says. "Especially to me."

"I think if he'd died then, I wouldn't have had so much time after to fall more in love with him and get hurt. I wouldn't have given my whole heart or slept with him. I didn't know how much it would hurt physically or mentally."

"Do you think losing him would have been easier if you hadn't been intimate with him?"

"Maybe. I don't know, really. I do know I wouldn't have given him my virginity if I hadn't loved him. That part was always important to me. I guess I didn't consider I needed to wait for someone who loved me. It didn't matter how much I loved him. It wasn't enough."

"Did Jason tell you he loved you?"

I shake my head. "He never said he did or didn't. He kept coming around even after saying we shouldn't be together and that I couldn't possibly love him so soon. It pissed me off when he kept telling me how I should feel. It made me want to tell him even more. Like I had to convince him he was worthy of love."

Dr. Benson looks at me, then writes a quick note on the pad in her hand. "So, what I'm hearing is you felt like you had to keep telling him how you felt to prove him worthy or was it to convince him you were worthy? Is it possible he made you so angry you were determined to prove him wrong and latched on to those feelings? Even if the feelings might have naturally faded over time given the way he treated you?"

I scoff. "Now you're telling me I don't know how I felt. How I feel? Like it's so easy to fall out of love?"

"That's not what I'm saying. I believe you still love Jason."

"I'll always love him."

"If it were a perfect world, and you and Jason could be together again. Would you want it?"

"No." I don't need to think about my answer.

"And why is that?"

"I need more than love; there has to be trust too. And I could never trust him not to leave me again. I'm heartbroken, but I'm not delusional. I'm strong enough now to know why he and I didn't work, and I'm scared I'll never love anyone as much when or if I fall in love again. Isn't that what all the poets say, the first one is always the hardest?"

"Do you love yourself, Lydia?"

"I try to."

"What about trust? Do you trust yourself?"

"Sometimes. Following my heart sure did lead me into a lot of hurt. And I'm afraid of repeating it with someone else. I was so stupid with Jason. I ignored all the red flags and my friends' warnings. I was so delusional with love that I honestly thought I would be his exception. That he'd suddenly realize he couldn't live without me, and we'd be happy forever. It sounds ridiculous."

Dr. Benson nods to acknowledge me, and I tell her about Kolton and what things he now knows about me.

With a small smile, Dr. Benson looks up from her notebook and sets the pen down. "Is Kolton this 'someone else' who might be a possibility?"

I smile at the thought of Kolton's warm eyes. "Maybe a chance. There was a kiss we had to do as part of the acting workshop, and Kolton told me afterward he wanted to kiss me again without the audience. He wants to go out on a date."

"Tell me about your feelings after it happened."

"I cried and told him I was too messed up to think about dating right now. Kolton said there was no pressure, but all I feel is pressure. And I'm lonely, starved for company. I like him; I know I do, but I don't want to date him for the wrong reasons."

"What are you going to do with those feelings?"

"I guess I'm going to continue to get to know him better and see what happens. I don't know what else to do except take it as it comes, at a snail's pace."

"It sounds like you have a plan."

For once, I'm among the first few people to get to the acting workshop on Thursday. Kolton's nowhere to be seen, and as soon as I sit down in my usual spot, Nel arrives and walks over.

"Hey, girl," she says. "What's up with you?"

"Nothing much," I say. "How are you?"

"Ah, I'm fine. Our lunch crew discussed you and Kolton after class. We figured you two might be off alone continuing kissing practice."

I'm glad the lighting on the stage hides the color in my cheeks. "Kolton and I are just friends, and the kissing was acting. Same as yours was with Tom."

"I see," she says, "But my kiss with Tom was nowhere near as hot as the one between you and Kolton. The rest of us are taking bets on how long it will be before you two are together...or at least hooking up."

"Seriously? Don't you all have anything better to talk about?"

"Nope. I think we're all romantics at heart, except you, I guess. But I bet even you can't deny the chemistry."

"Well, you heard Kolton talking about his ex. I don't think he's in any position to date, and I have my own shit going on. Dating would probably be a disaster." I'm not completely convinced we shouldn't try though. Maybe it could work out.

"Oh, so you have considered taking it to another 'position' with him. Interesting." She looks up and then stands to head back to her seat.

Soon, Kolton is standing in front of me. "This seat taken?" he asks with a smile.

"It's all yours," I say, smiling back at him. "I am your partner and all."

He sighs and takes a seat. "It's been a crazy week so far."

"What's up?"

"A lot's going on with my family. Could we grab some food after class? Just us? I could use a friend."

I look up to see his sincerity and instantly agree. Behind him, Nel is giving me double thumbs-up signs. I shake my head at her.

"You should know the others are shipping us hard," I tell Kolton. "They have bets going and everything."

"Nice to be famous." He laughs. "Maybe we should go out already to give the people what they want."

"We'll see."

When Bernetta starts the workshop, I notice she's watching Kolton and me more than any of the other partner groups. After the morning exercises, she asks to see us as she dismisses the class for lunch.

She waits until the stage is clear to speak to us in a hushed tone. "I wanted to talk to you two alone about the auditions," she says. "We'll, of course, go through the formal process for casting the leads and supporting cast, but right now, I have my eyes on the two of you for my leads. The amount of passion for the craft I see in each of you is remarkable, and you two also have some natural chemistry that can't be faked even by the most talented actors."

"W-wow," Kolton stutters. "Thank you so much."

"Yes," I say. "Thank you."

"Are you both committed to giving this play your all?" she asks. "Because this is a wonderful opportunity to get out there."

"I am," I say and turn to Kolton. He looks a little peaked all of a sudden.

"Yeah, yeah," he says. "I'm here to earn the role if I can."

"You can," Bernetta says to him and then turns to me. "And so can you."

I drive us to the diner to find my regular lunch order sitting at my spot in the booth and so is Kolton's. Tom, Nel, Jake, and Tanya are laughing as the two of us slip into our seats.

"Did Bernetta tell you guys to tone it down and stop making the rest of us look bad?" Tom asks. "If either of you could suck a bit, it would make me feel a little better."

Nel pinches his arm. "Shut up, Tommy boy," she says. "They're doing great."

Kolton chuckles. "Thanks for your confidence in us, Nel."

She winks at me. "No problem. Tom's just jelly."

"I don't even want a lead role," Tanya says. "I've always felt more like a supporting role kinda gal. And I don't think there's anything wrong with that. I even told Bernetta that last week."

"Me neither," Jake says, rubbing his head. "I've never wanted the pressure of carrying the show."

"Well," Tom says. "I love being in the spotlight whether it's lead or supporting, serious or comic relief. I played Puck in my university's Shakespeare production my senior year."

"I can see you as Puck," Kolton says.

"It's hard to know what role I want to try for until we get to see the script," Nel says. "We really have no idea since the description is so vague and mysterious."

"We'll know soon enough," I say. "I like having something to look forward to."

For dinner, Kolton and I return to the diner and sit in a booth for two. He orders a breakfast meal and doesn't laugh when I order a grilled cheese from the kid's menu.

"What's going on with your family?" I ask as he fiddles with his sugar packet wrapper.

"Well, Kendra decided to make a couple of life changes that aren't sitting well with our parents. One, she's moving to San Francisco, and two, she's getting married to her girlfriend of four years."

"Oh wow."

"Yeah, I'm not sure whether my parents are more upset about the move or the wedding. Although, she's planning to go to the courthouse. A lot of our parents' church friends wouldn't approve of a gay wedding anyway, so you'd think they'd be relieved. I guess it could be the move. They think California is a good place to get murdered."

"What will they think of you going on tour if this play works out?"

"They won't love it, but they seem to think having a penis makes me safer from murder like they expect me to whip it out like a sword to defend myself or something."

I can't help but laugh. "I hope you don't do too much whipping it around!"

Kolton raises his eyebrows and I blush. "Now you'll never get the image out of your head," he says with a chuckle.

It's now or never to talk to him. "Hey, about what you said the other day and today, about us dating..."

His smile drops instantly. "Too much too soon, right?"

"I honestly don't know. I know I like you, Kolton, but my ex did a number on me, and the worst part is, I'm mostly to blame for letting him. Dating again makes me nervous since I'm not over it yet."

"Not over him or not over the situation?"

"A little of both, I guess. I've been trying to sort everything out, but sometimes I feel more confused than ever."

"Do you want to get back together with him?" Kolton asks. "Would that make you happier?"

"It's not possible for me to get back together with him, and even if it were, I wouldn't. After everything that happened, I lost too much trust in him that could never be earned back, if that makes sense."

"It does. It's taken me a while to want to date again after my ex too. You're the first woman I've considered worth the risk of trying."

"I'm flattered, and I'm not saying I don't want to go out with you sometime, because I do. I just need a little more time to heal before I see anyone else romantically. I hope you understand. I enjoy hanging out with you and the others and when it's just us."

"I understand completely," he says simply. "I can't say I won't enjoy our kissing scenes in the meantime, though."

"They're not the worst part of my day," I tease. "It's not fair to you when I know I'm not one hundred percent."

"I feel like I operate at seventy-five on a good day."

"Well, I'm shooting for eighty, so look out."

Chapter 18
October 18, 2019

I lived like a zombie for the next week. I avoided doing anything outside of going to class and Art Club, but when I was there, I wished I were somewhere else. Anywhere else. Being around Jason was excruciating. He barely looked at me, but I couldn't stop sneaking peeks at him. He looked a bit rough like he hadn't shaved since I'd last seen him.

Of course, I knew I looked bad too. I didn't wear makeup all week because it was pointless. In between classes and at night, I'd cry. It was inevitable. Each time I tried to distract myself, I'd start thinking of Jason again. It was a wonder I managed to get through my assignments at all. Marienne had stayed close to me each evening after finding me sobbing in the dorm the Sunday after the breakup with her "asshole cousin." I dreaded Friday night coming around again since she had to work.

My mom expected me to come home Saturday morning and stay the night since Luke would be there to visit. I worried she'd be able to see right through everything I'd hidden over the phone. I had to see her at some point and prove how talented my acting could be. Of course, Luke would probably know something was wrong when I didn't want to talk about college at all. Everything was all tied up with how I felt about Jason and having lost him.

When the familiar sound of tapping on my window Friday evening jarred me from my recurring nightmare of Jason dying, I was crying by the time I raised the blinds. I pulled open the window and let Jason step through. He closed the window behind him and turned around. Upon seeing my tears, he pulled me into his arms.

"Hey, what's wrong?" he whispered.

"I miss you," I whimpered. "I keep having dreams I can't save you, and it's the most terrible thing I can imagine. And you completely ignored me in Art Club. It hurts."

"I'm not gone," he said, pulling away to sit on my bed. "I don't want to hurt you. I didn't think you'd be ready to talk to me right after the meeting. I wanted to give you some space to think."

"Jason, I want the opposite of space with you." I turned to the sink next to the bathroom that connected my room to another and ran water over a washrag. I wiped my face, but there was no disguising I was an ugly crier.

"Come sit with me," Jason said, patting the bed.

I joined him and pulled my legs to my chest, trying to hide that I wasn't wearing a bra under my ratty old t-shirt. "What did you want to talk about?"

"I've decided I'm not drinking anymore. I think what happened was the kick in the ass I needed to work through a few things."

"You don't know how happy it makes me to hear that, Jason. I was worried about you."

"Don't. My parents are riding my ass about it and trying to get me to go to a rehab center. I don't need that though. I know I took it too far and need some time to let my mind and my body reset."

"So that's it? You don't need any help to stop drinking?"

"I'm not an addict or an alcoholic or anything. I like to escape and party sometimes. I don't have to do it. It wasn't fun waking up in the hospital with a tube stuck down my throat."

"It wasn't fun being on the other side either, not knowing if you were going to wake up at all. And it's not fun having nightmares every damn night about losing you, either."

"I'm not lost. I'm right here." He unlocks my arms and drags me closer until we're lying together, his head on my pillow.

When he tried to pull me even closer, I resisted for a moment. "Jason, your ribs."

"I'm fine," he said, bringing my head to his chest. His heart was pounding, and mine sped up to match his. "I think I should do some things differently since I've been given a second chance."

"That's good," I said. I wanted to cry again being close to him, but I managed to close my eyes and enjoy the moment.

"So, you really don't want space from me, do you? You want to keep dating even after what happened at the party and with me leaving the country in January?"

"I want to keep seeing you."

"I want to keep seeing you too."

It was all I wanted to hear, and the sense of relief I felt was almost too much to take.

"I have a question," he said after a couple of minutes of silence.

"What?"

"Are you still wanting to have sex with me?"

At that moment, I could have answered many different ways but 'yes' was the only truth I had. All through high school, I'd been obsessed with my eventual first time and also terrified of it. Now that it was right in front of me, I felt ready to go through with it. I was sure I loved him, so it was all I needed.

"You sure?" he asked, using his thumbs to wipe the remaining tears off my cheeks.

"I am." To prove it to him, I got up and found the bag of condoms the health department had given me when I'd gotten my birth control prescription. I pulled one out and placed it on the bed beside us. It was all the permission he needed.

Though we'd fooled around a lot, it was the first time we'd seen each other completely naked—well except for the tight bandage around Jason's ribs. I wasn't self-conscious; I wanted every part of him as close to me as possible.

As ready as I thought I was to have sex, I wasn't prepared for how much it would hurt, the intense pressure followed by burning pain like I was being torn apart from the outside in.

"Do you want me to stop?" Jason whispered, and I realized I was crying again, only out loud.

"No. I'm okay." I wasn't, but I didn't want our togetherness to end. It would get better, right? Otherwise, why the hell would anyone ever do it more than once?

When Jason got up, I stayed down, feeling sore and damp. I closed my eyes as I sat up, afraid to look at myself. "I think I'm bleeding."

"Here," Jason said, grabbing the roll of paper towels near my sink. He tore off a couple before tossing the roll to me and used them to remove the condom, which was glazed with blood. My blood.

I took some towels for myself and stuffed them between my legs as I searched for my panties. After I found them, I stood up and pulled them on to keep the wadded paper towels in place.

"Isn't that uncomfortable?" he asked, watching me as he dressed.

I felt about as far away from sexy as humanly possible. I yanked my shirt back over my head, not caring it was inside out. "It's fine," I said, and then I started pulling my sheet off the bed since it was also stained with blood. I was mortified. Not knowing what to do with it, I rolled the sheet into a ball and stuffed it into the sink.

Jason was tying his shoes when I turned around, but I didn't know what to say to him. He looked at me and then stood up. "I have to go," he said, walking closer to look into my eyes. "You okay?"

"Yeah, I'm fine," I told him. He hugged me and pressed his lips to my forehead as I wrapped my arms around him. His heart had slowed down since earlier. I watched him open the window and climb outside and followed to close and lock it behind him.

As soon as he was gone, I went to the bathroom to clean myself up. After a quick shower, I was still bleeding, so I dug a pad out of my stash to save my panties. Once I'd dressed, I pulled the bottle of hydrogen peroxide out of my first aid kit and used the whole thing trying to save my sheets.

I watched as the bubbles attacked the stains and wondered if I'd made a mistake. Wasn't sex supposed to be romantic? Because what I'd just done was nothing like I'd seen in movies.

Chapter 19
June 22, 2024

It's Saturday, and I have a rare day off work, so I let myself sleep in for once. I don't have any plans until lunch, and I'm startled awake when Mom knocks on my door and then lets herself in.

"Not working today?"

"Not today," I say, stretching as I sit up in bed. "One of my coworkers needed the extra money, so I let her have my shift."

"It's good to have a break," she says, sitting by my feet. "I'm taking the day off too. Any plans?"

"I thought I'd hang out here today, maybe read or watch a couple of movies. And I'm meeting Phoebe for lunch."

"That's good. Maybe you and I can do something together this afternoon."

"Sure, that sounds great."

Mom rests her hand on my leg. "I'm glad you're still seeing Dr. Benson."

"I still have a lot of things to work on, but I know I'll get better eventually. Don't worry about me, please." I wasn't sure what level of better I could be, but I had hope.

"I can't help but worry about you after last year and with the anniversary of the accident having passed." She moves closer and grabs my shoulders. "Lydia, you'd tell me if you were having suicidal thoughts again, wouldn't you?"

I look into her eyes, which are about to spill over, and have to turn away so I won't cry with her. "I promise, I'm not, even with the anniversary. The workshop has been good to give me something exciting to focus on."

"But are you okay?" she asks, wiping away her tears. "Almost losing you last year was the scariest time of my life. I'm thankful every day you're still here with us. I don't think I could survive losing you, Lydia."

"I'm really sorry, Mom. I won't ever let myself get to that dark place again. I didn't want to die; I just wanted it to stop. All the hurting. Marienne. Jason. It'd gotten to be too much."

"I wish I could take away all the pain, but I can't. All I can do is keep reminding you you're meant to be in this world, baby. You're going to do fabulous things. I just know it."

"I hope you're right," I say, leaning forward to hug her.

She squeezes me so much I can hardly breathe, but I don't want to leave the warmth of her embrace. "I know I'm right. Your dad and your grandparents would be so proud of you for taking a chance with the workshop and audition."

"Thanks for telling me that. I wish I could remember more about Dad." And it's true. My memories of my dad feel like almost forgotten dreams—fuzzy at the edges and surreal. The most vivid one is an image of him at the funeral, lying still in his casket surrounded by the most beautiful, fragrant flowers I'd ever encountered at the time. Everyone around me cried, but I was too confused to understand why my father was in a box and Mom had told me he wouldn't be coming home anymore.

"Anytime you have a question about him, ask me. I'll do my best to fill in the gaps."

"I've never wanted to make you sad by talking about him."

"Loss is part of life, unfortunately. The sadness becomes part of us, but it doesn't have to break us. I miss him, but I also know he wouldn't want me to be miserable. Maybe Marienne and...well maybe they both feel the same way about you. They'd want you to live your life and be happy."

"I know. It's hard and there are days when I wonder if I'll ever be completely happy again. There's still this huge gap in my heart like part of my soul is missing. I thought Jason was my soulmate, and maybe the universe is trying to tell me I'm not supposed to have anyone romantically."

Mom sniffs and clenches her eyes shut for a moment. "Oh, Lyddie," she says, looking at me again. "I don't believe that. I think sometimes, people are put into our lives to be soul guides rather than soulmates. These people change us and prepare us for what's to come. It doesn't mean love wasn't there or real, it just means the relationship wasn't meant to last a lifetime. Perhaps it was too intense or too fragile, but the souls crossed paths for a reason—a lesson or the creation of a beautiful daughter like you—a reason we don't always understand until we're older and maybe never."

So much for not crying. I'm in tears now and my jaws ache from trying to hold off my emotions for so long.

At noon, I meet Phoebe at our favorite pizza place. She's already inside when I get there and waves from a booth near the middle of the restaurant. As I take my seat across from her, I realize she's about to burst with some news she wants to tell me.

I chuckle, "Okay, out with it!"

She smiles even more and puts her left hand out on the table. On her ring finger is a gold band adorned with a blue sapphire surrounded by a halo of diamonds. From the look in her eyes, I know it's more than new jewelry—it's the promise of continued love, and I'm so thrilled for her I think my heart my burst.

"Wow...it's beautiful," I say, swallowing a lump in my throat.

"Sam asked me last night," she squeals. "I wanted to tell you in person."

I get up to hug her and start crying as soon as my arms wrap around her. "Congratulations."

"Oh, Lyds, please don't cry. It breaks my heart."

"I can't help it! I'm so happy for you two." I pull from her embrace and return to my seat. Giving up on my makeup, I dry my face with the cloth napkin on the table. "When's the big day?"

"We're still figuring it out, but we're thinking the end of the summer, late August, or early September. Something small in my parents' backyard. We've been together long enough we don't see the need for a long engagement."

"That sounds amazing."

"I wanted to ask you to be my maid of honor."

"Yes. Of course."

"Yay! If you still have that amazing red dress you wore to our senior prom, I'd love for you to wear it."

"It's in the closet. I kept telling myself I might wear it again, and now I guess I will!"

The waiter arrives to take our order, and then we start discussing the workshop after Phoebe insists we've talked enough about her. I tell her more stories about the interesting people I've met and how excited I am about the upcoming audition.

"I can't wait to hear you've got the lead part," she says. "Maybe I can fly out to see you for a show."

"I think there will be a show in Little Rock. Plus, it's not guaranteed I'll get the lead, despite what Bernetta said, but the odds are good I'll at least get some part. Of course, I hope Kolton gets the lead too."

Phoebe grins and then winks at me. "There's another mention of Kolton. I think you might like him a little."

"Well, he's interested in going out with me."

"And? Are you going to?"

"I'm not looking for romance right now, but maybe someday."

"There's no time like the present. Maybe give someone a chance and don't hold him to impossible standards."

"What's that supposed to mean?" But I already know.

"You still have Jason up on a pedestal in your heart, and until you let him go, I'm afraid you're holding yourself back and missing out on the potential of another relationship—when you're ready, of course. I know you've been through a lot, but I love you so much, and damn it, you deserve to be swept off your feet by someone who's truly worthy of you."

My eyes sting and I can hardly speak until Phoebe reaches out and takes my hand. "Thank you."

"I'm being honest," she says, squeezing my hand before releasing it. "Just like I'm going to expect you to be honest and the voice of reason when I'm shopping for wedding dresses with my mother. Don't let me cave to what she likes and speak up about what's most flattering on me."

"You bet."

The waiter arrives with our pizza just in time to stop the emotional conversation. I cut my slice up with a knife and fork to get it to cool quickly so I won't scald the roof of my mouth. Phoebe's always been my most honest friend, even when the truth hurts. And she's right this time as well; I have had Jason up on a pedestal.

The truth is he made me feel bad about myself more often than he made me feel good. It's tough to accept that, but I'll have to if I ever want to move on and let someone else into my life in that way. The main problem is I'm terrified of getting hurt again and worried I'm not strong enough to handle it when or if I do. Because—let's face it—I can't guarantee the next guy I love will be the love of my life and feel the same way about me.

When we're done eating, I hug Phoebe goodbye, marvel once again about how happy I am for her and Sam, and then drop into my car. I wonder what my mother has planned for our together time this afternoon. I need to keep myself distracted. As I start my car, my phone connects to the sound system and immediately rings with Kolton's contact info displaying.

"Hey, Kolton."

"Hey, Lydia, sounds like you're in your car."

"Yeah." I buckle my seatbelt and put the car into gear. From the noise on the line, I can tell he's driving too. "I'm leaving from lunch with my friend Phoebe. She's getting married at the end of the summer."

"Oh wow. Don't you have another friend getting married soon too?"

"Yep. I get the distinct pleasure of being a maid of honor in two weddings this summer." I leave the parking lot and head back toward my parents' house.

"Sounds a bit more involved than me being a witness at my sister's wedding."

"Probably. I'm happy for Vicki and Phoebe, but I'll have to admit I'm a bit jealous."

"I'm not jealous of Kendra's wedding, but it's what she and her girlfriend want. I'd want something more personal for my own wedding."

"It's not the weddings I'm jealous of, it's that they're both marrying their first real boyfriends and didn't have to go through broken hearts to get there."

Kolton's quiet for a moment, and I think the call's dropped before he speaks again. "I'm sorry. I can see how it would be hard for you with everything you've been through in the past year."

"I'll get through it. I have to."

"Well, if you need a friend or a wedding date, or both, I'm here for you."

"I appreciate it." I pull to a stop at a red light and notice the couple in the car next to me laughing. I'm constantly reminded of a relationship I want and don't have. "What are you up to today?"

"Not much. I'm driving now to help my dad install some custom cabinets at his friend's house. I'm hoping I'll get through it without losing my shit. The guy is one of the more vocal ones from the church and has a strong opinion about Kendra."

"I'm surprised the guy would want your family in his house. Isn't having a gay family member contagious?"

Kolton chuckles, "See? That's why I called you. I knew you could make me feel better."

"Glad to help. Just keep the tools to yourself, and you should be fine."

"Maybe I should use my sword. The dude would probably lose his mind."

"I don't think getting naked around power tools is the best way to go, but you do you!" Now I have him laughing. "You're way too obsessed with your favorite tool."

"I only mentioned a sword. You're the one who made the penis association. For all you know, I could have a Samurai sword hanging on my wall."

He's right, I did make the connection. "I don't know what to say."

"It's totally fine with you picturing me in the nude now. I'm not modest. But anyway, I need to go. Thanks for brightening my day."

"Same to you."

I'm smiling by the time I arrive back home and catch my mom on her way out the door. She's dressed in a pantsuit and heels.

"I thought you were taking the day off."

"I am, officially," she tells me. "But another realtor's sick and can't show a listing that's been on the market forever, so I told her I'd take care of it. I'll be back soon and insist you let me take you with me for a manicure. No excuses!"

I glance down at my nails, worn down from my awful habit of chewing them. "Fine. I'll do it."

When she's gone, I realize it's the first time since my suicide attempt Mom has demanded I go with her to the salon. She used to make me go all the time when I was in high school to help me keep my nails healthy and also to make sure I was talking to her regularly. Back then, it frustrated me, but now I'm thankful.

Chapter 20
October 28, 2019

My time wasn't my own anymore. It was all Jason's. We had sex again in the back seat of my car at a secluded park after he'd agreed to pose for my sketch for the figure drawing lesson in my art class. It wasn't much better than the first time, but at least I didn't bleed again.

The third time in a supply closet in the Art Building late at night wasn't painful at all, except emotionally since he got a text and had to leave right afterward.

The fourth time, back in my dorm room, was good. We weren't rushed since Marienne was staying with her parents for the weekend. Jason stayed and held me for a while before he had to go. It was what I really wanted—to feel loved. I lost track of the times and places soon enough.

The problem was, when I wasn't with Jason, I was thinking about being with him again. But what I missed more than anything wasn't the connection between our bodies—I longed for more conversations. I wanted our minds to connect as much—if not more—than our bodies.

But I worried I wouldn't see him at all if sex wasn't part of the deal. Even worse was that I was afraid to talk to anyone about it. I didn't want one of my friends to tell me Jason was using me, even if deep down in my heart I felt it.

I still saw Vicki and Marienne at lunch every day, but I hadn't spoken with Phoebe in ages. She called one afternoon when I had just settled into my bed for a nap after classes.

"Hey, stranger," I answered. "How have you been?"

"I should ask you that! It's like you've fallen off the face of the earth. I thought you were coming home every couple of weekends, and we might have time to catch up."

"I'm so sorry! I've had a lot of homework and studying to do to keep up."

"I understand. So...how are things with Jason?"

"We're fine."

"Just fine? It's been a couple of months now, right? Did you two make it official?"

"I don't know...kind of."

"What do you mean?"

I started picking at a stray thread on my pillowcase. I had to talk to someone, and she'd known me longer than my other friends. "It's complicated. He's not wanting a girlfriend right now, so it's not official in that sense. I was upset at first, but I think we've worked through it."

"How complicated does it need to be?" she asked. "Either you're together or you're not. He needs to man up or you need to cut him loose."

"He's studying abroad next year and doesn't want to be in a serious relationship, and I get it, I guess. Plus, he's under a lot of pressure both from his parents and with his classes."

"Life has pressure, Lydia. How do you feel about him, I mean really? Is seeing him worth it if it isn't going anywhere?"

I couldn't answer her at first as I choked back tears. Maybe it wasn't going anywhere, but the thought of letting him go broke my heart.

"Lydia? You still there?"

I tried to hide the sob stuck in my throat but failed miserably. "He got alcohol poisoning a few weeks back, and the last thing I want to do is add more pressure to what he's already going through. It was awful having him almost die in my arms, and I love him enough to do what I can to be here for him."

Phoebe gasps. "Oh, girlie, you love him? Are you sure? Have you told him?"

Letting my tears fall, I break and tell her everything, including how I don't want to feel used for sex, but it's the only way I feel close to him anymore.

"Wow," she says after several seconds of silence. "That's a lot to deal with. I love you, Lydia, you know I do, so please know I say this with love—you deserve better. You should have someone who wants to be with you for real and not in secret only when it's convenient for him. None of this is fair to you since you're clearly not up for the 'hook-up buddy' arrangement he's made."

"I know." By that point, I'd unraveled the entire seam of my pillowcase and cried a month's worth of tears.

"I have to go to class now but promise me you'll talk to him. Don't hook up just because he wants to. Your feelings matter too."

"Thank you for letting me unload all this stuff on you."

"Love ya, girl."

"Love you too."

I woke up about an hour later when Marienne came in after class closely followed by Vicki. "I'm sorry," she whispered. "I didn't mean to wake you."

"It's fine. I don't need to sleep all day."

With that, she turned on the overhead light and took a good look at me. "It looks like you've been crying again. What's going on?"

"Just having a rough day. I was on the phone with my friend Phoebe, and everything came out."

"Let me guess, it has something to do with my dickhead cousin being his dickhead self?"

I looked down at my hands. It's hard to say anything bad about Jason, especially to his cousin, but I hadn't said anything as bad as what Marienne had said herself. She climbed onto my bed and took my hands while Vicki plopped down in my desk chair.

"Don't let him treat you like crap just because you love him," Vicki said. "You deserve better."

"That's what Phoebe said too."

"You don't seem very happy lately, Lydia," Marienne said. "Please tell us what's going on with Jason. He's been avoiding me lately."

I told them everything, and the more I unloaded, the lighter I felt. Of course, saying it all out loud again made me see a few things differently. I asked myself what I would do if Phoebe or Vicki or Marienne were experiencing the same thing with someone one of them were dating—what would I tell them? I'd tell them to stand up for themselves, and it was exactly what I would have to do unless I wanted to stay miserable and let myself feel so used.

"I think I have a messed-up view of sex...and love," I tell Dr. Benson during our early morning session. "I've only been with Jason, and you see how that ended. I always wanted to save myself for love, and I did, but I got so caught up in the moment of how I felt I failed to remember I should have made sure he felt the same way so the whole thing wouldn't end in a disaster."

Dr. Benson nods her head and takes some quick notes. "Disasters have a way of teaching us things we couldn't learn otherwise. Please, continue."

"I wanted Jason to love me so badly I lost a lot of myself along the way. I did things I knew weren't right—for me anyway—but I kept having sex with him because it was the only time I felt loved and close to him. Until he'd up and leave and then ignore me until he wanted to have sex again. I struggled with saying 'no' to him, and then when I finally developed enough courage to tell him what I wanted, I let him manipulate me into doing what he wanted. I let him. Looking back, I'm still so angry."

"Angry at Jason or yourself?"

"Both, but mostly me. I should've known better."

She puts down her pen and leans toward me. "But how? How would you have known better if it was your first relationship and your first time feeling that way? Your feelings weren't necessarily wrong even if you feel differently now. It's all about growth, Lydia. And forgiveness. You've said many times you forgive Jason for hurting you during your relationship, but I've never heard you say you forgive yourself for your part in all of it. Sometimes it's the hardest part of moving on—forgiving ourselves for mistakes we've made and things we've allowed to happen that in turn made us feel bad about ourselves."

"I'm scared."

Dr. Benson leans back in her chair, crossing her legs, waiting for me to go on.

"I'm afraid of never loving anyone again like I loved Jason. And I'm also afraid I will and will keep getting hurt again and again until there's nothing left of me. I'm terrified I'll end up in a scary place again where I want to end my life to stop the pain. What if I'm not strong enough? Am I better off swearing off men and staying single and lonely to protect my heart? Why does it have to be so hard? I mean, people have been pairing up since the beginning of time."

"Philosophers and poets have also been trying to figure out love since the beginning of recorded history, Lydia. You've made so much progress over the last year. I know you're strong, and it's only natural to doubt yourself as you're coming to terms with your feelings. Your truth will come, and it might hurt while it heals you. You're a strong enough woman to work through everything and come out the other side a changed version of yourself—the self you've been searching for this whole time. She's always been there, hidden under the fear and hurt you've been through since you were a child."

"You think losing my dad when I was so young started some of my problems?"

"We should explore it further next week."

I agree and grab my purse to leave, anxious to get to the cemetery.

I drive on autopilot and arrive at the cemetery before I realize how quickly the time has passed. As I approach Marienne's grave, I see Jason sitting on the bench. I crouch to place the flowers near the headstone and then get up to sit beside him. I don't say anything, but I feel him looking at the side of my face.

My heart is torn between wanting to hug him and wanting to punch him in the throat.

We sit for a while, not talking. It's grueling having millions of feelings—most of them conflicting—and being unable to find the words to express them. I wish I could erase all the pain from Jason and keep only the good memories. It's easier to fantasize than make it a reality.

"I didn't do a good job of showing you I cared about you," Jason says after a few more minutes of silence. "A lot of it was being scared to commit to anyone when there was still so much I wanted to do. I didn't want anyone to hold me back, and at the same time, I didn't want to hold anyone else back either. I didn't want to hold you back."

"And oddly enough, I wanted you to hold me more than anything else sometimes. That or have a deep conversation like we did when we first went out. I had sex with you to feel closer to you since I loved you. I'll never understand how anyone can separate sex from feelings."

"Sex and love aren't the same thing."

"I know they're not the same. I can't understand sharing something so intimate with someone you don't love. I never would have given you that part of myself if I hadn't been in love with you. Hell, I wouldn't be talking to you now if I didn't still love you. And I don't understand because, thinking back on everything that happened between us and how you treated me sometimes, I don't like you very much."

"It was by design. I was being an ass to try to make you hate me."

"Maybe I'm the ass. The only person I hated was myself. I kept chasing you because I was so desperate for someone to love me. I thought if you didn't feel anything for me then nobody would. It's taken me a long time to come to terms with that."

"I want you to heal, Lydia. We just weren't meant to be together for very long."

His insistence on being right was always the biggest pain point for me during our disaster of a relationship. I'd been so frantic to prove my love for him I'd lost chunks of my soul in the process. Looking at him now, I wonder if I truly loved him or if I was as stubborn as he was with the desire to be right about my feelings.

Looking back, I'm mortified at how I'd chased him, but I can't go back and change things. There are a lot of things I'd change if I could, like preventing the car accident. I'd give anything to stop it. "I thought you were my soulmate, Jason. I'd never felt such a connection to another person before, and I don't know if I ever will. I thought I'd die without you, and I almost did."

"I'm glad you didn't. You're going to do great things. I always knew that."

"Sometimes I wish we never met, Jason. Then maybe I wouldn't miss you so damn much. Then there are other times I wonder if it's really you I miss or if I miss the person I was before you. I hope I'm stronger though, for having known you for a little while. I feel stronger than I did last year after the accident. I think Marienne would have been disappointed in me for wallowing in self-pity for so long."

"She'd want you to keep living. To go after the dreams she couldn't. She'd be right there with you in the workshop going after something big. Even though my cousin loved you more than she loved me, I knew her from the time she was born. I think she's looking out for you, Lydia. She'd want you to have everything and be happy."

"Thank you for saying that."

"Maybe I'm trying to look out for you too."

He's right, as much as it pains me to acknowledge it since I spent so long trying to convince him he was wrong about the two of us being unable to work long-term. Marienne would want me to keep living, and I feel like I've made strides in that with the workshop and the new friendships with the other actors, Kolton especially.

"What about you, Jason? What do you want?"

"I want you to have everything too, Lydia. Everything you've ever dreamed of."

"What about for yourself?"

"That, I don't know." He looks off in the distance.

"And what if I can't have everything? What if I can't have what I want most?"

"You have to believe there's something amazing out there for you. I know it's true."

"I guess I have a lot to think about." I stand to leave. "I'll see you next time, but I don't know how much longer I can keep talking to you. Sometimes it hurts me more than it helps."

Jason doesn't speak, and by the time I'm back to my car and glance back at the bench, he's gone.

Kolton calls as soon as my phone connects in my car, and I smile as I answer. "Hey, what's up?"

"I'm up to my eyeballs in cabinets that need staining. My dad had to take an emergency job with his new helper, so I said I'd fill in, but I didn't realize how big the job was. At this rate, I'll be here all night. You've painted sets before, haven't you? I need help if you're not busy. I can give you half the pay for the job."

"I've done quite a bit of set painting," I tell him. "And what are friends for? I can help, and I don't expect you to pay me."

"Awesome, and I insist on paying you for the work. I'm texting you the address now for my dad's workshop."

It pops up, and I see it's less than an hour away. I tell him I'm on the way and set out, calling my mom as I drive so she won't worry about me. I realize I'm excited to hang out with Kolton again.

Chapter 22
November 1, 2019

Taking a chance at standing up for myself, I ignored Jason's text on a Friday night when he wanted to hook up. After I saw the message come through, I closed the notification without replying in favor of hanging out with Vicki and Marienne. I needed some girl time to think so I could be strong enough to not be available anytime he wanted.

The three of us decided to drive around the backroads near the college while singing loudly to our favorite songs. Marienne and I were used to singing on stage, but Vicki shocked us with her sweet voice rocking along to her favorite boy band hits. We left Russellville and traveled through several small towns like Blue Ball, Mount George, and later on, a town called Chickalah after we'd passed Dardanelle on the other side of the Arkansas River.

Vicki drove an older extended cab pickup truck with folding back seats, and since I was shorter than Marienne, I volunteered to sit in the smaller space. It wasn't bad since I could rest my head against the cool window and look up at the stars once it was dark enough and we were away from streetlights.

I hated to admit I missed Jason, but I did. I was torn between being free and being captivated by the thought of his touch. Sex or a conversation. I'd have taken either because what I wanted more than anything was for him to take me in his arms and tell me he loved me and couldn't live another minute without me being his forever. And I knew how crazy I sounded in my head, but he'd captured my heart with his vulnerability that night at the party. The connection I felt to him was stronger than any logic I could throw at my feelings.

Being with him wasn't the problem. With him, I felt like I could be happy forever. The after was when the doubt set in.

When he barely acknowledged me during Art Club meetings. When he always had to leave right after we'd had sex. During those moments I felt cheap and used. But then he'd show up again and brush my hair from my forehead, and I was a goner. Hopelessly in love with him.

Marienne's voice breaks through, and I notice the music isn't on anymore. "Lydia, you better not be back there thinking about him."

"I'm trying not to," I said. "I ignored his text wanting to see me tonight. What more can I do?"

"Dump his ass," Vicki said. "He's using you."

"Maybe we're using each other since I've wanted a boyfriend for so long." I knew it wasn't true the moment the words left my mouth.

"Ha!" Marienne said. "That's the dumbest thing I've ever heard you say."

"Maybe I'm dumb then! I slept with him without a real commitment because I love him. I just want him to love me back. What's wrong with that?"

"There's nothing wrong with wanting love, Lydia," Vicki said. "But..."

"But what?"

"But he doesn't love you," Marienne said. "Or if he does somewhere deep inside, he's being a dumbass about it and stringing you along, Lydia. It's not fair, and I know it hurts, but you will find a guy who can appreciate how amazing you are. He's out there, but I don't think his name is Jason Allan Caldwell."

"Exactly," Vicki said.

They thought they were right about everything and were trying to look out for me. I knew it, but my heart wasn't connecting with my head at all.

I finally texted Jason when I got back to the dorm, and it was after three in the morning by that time. He didn't respond right away, so I went to bed. When I woke up later in the day, Marienne had already left for work, and I noticed Jason had read my message about an hour before and wanted to hang out later.

When I suggested going out somewhere to eat, he offered to bring burgers with him instead so we could eat in the Art Building since he needed to work on some projects. It wasn't exactly what I wanted to do, but I relented because I missed him. Plus, if he was working, we might have more of a chance to talk since his hands would be busy.

I was already in the building working on the shading for my still-life drawing when Jason arrived with our food. He put it down on the empty table beside me and took a seat. I got up to wash the graphite off my hands and came back to find him already eating, and my food was sitting across from him.

He nodded in my direction and swallowed the food in his mouth as I sat down. "How's the drawing coming along?" he asked, reaching for more fries.

"It's fine," I said. "I'm having a little trouble with the shading, but I think I'll get it if I work at it long enough."

"Good shading makes a difference when you're working in monochrome."

"Sorry I missed your text last night."

Jason shrugged. "I hung out with Mack most of the night. He's upset his ex-wife won't let their son come to his house. And Lila's pissed off too because she thinks it's all about her."

"How old's his son?"

"Three or four."

"I know he's your friend, but I can't blame his ex. The place isn't really...well, there was a bong on the table and all the liquor bottles."

"Those were there for the party. He doesn't have stuff out all the time. I don't judge him for smoking and drinking occasionally."

"It's not about being judgmental. I don't think his place is safe for kids. I mean, would you want your nieces hanging out there?"

Jason gets up, stuffs his wrappers into his paper bag, and wads it up before tossing it into the trash can. "I guess it isn't any of my business. Glad I don't have to deal with the bullshit of a girlfriend and an ex fighting. It's easier being unattached."

His words hit me like a punch in the gut. "Not everyone wants to be unattached, which is why I'm dating you."

"That's why you should've gone out with the guy at the carnival."

"What?"

"The face paint guy." Jason gestures toward his own face like I don't know who he's talking about.

He'd pissed me off and I lost my appetite for the rest of my food. "I know who you're talking about, but I don't think of him that way."

"He'd be your boyfriend. It's what you want, isn't it? A boyfriend? A relationship where you're not just dating casually."

"Like it's a role to be filled by anyone!"

"There are a lot of guys who'd be your boyfriend, Lydia." Jason crossed his arms and leaned against the doorframe.

"Where are you going with this?"

"You're not happy with our situation. You want a relationship I can't commit to right now."

"Of course, I'm not happy, Jason! It doesn't feel like we're actually dating, even casually. We never go anywhere. All you want to do is have sex with me or pick a fight with me. It's like you're hot and cold constantly."

For a moment, he looked truly hurt. "You know I'm leaving at the end of the year, and I was upfront about it. It seemed like we could...I don't know...use each other—"

"What!?!" I threw my hands up in the air. "I'm not using you. I'm trying to show you how much I love you."

"I enjoy having sex with you, and we can hook up until I leave, or you find someone else is what I'm saying."

I stood up and walked closer to him. "Are you joking right now? I'm not looking for anyone else because I'm in love with you. It's not like you're dropping off the face of the earth at the end of the year! You think you're not worth waiting for? That I can't be here for you when you come back?"

Jason looked at his feet, but he didn't say anything.

His silence felt like another punch to the gut, but I couldn't stop talking. "Or is it me? You don't think I'm worth waiting for?"

"What if I don't want to come back here? You're just getting started."

"I'll go wherever you go. I'm not tied to this town."

"You can't change everything and make all your decisions on emotions that may not even be—"

"Stop telling me I don't know how I feel! If I can't make my own decisions based on love, then what else is there? What's the purpose of life without love?"

"Logic."

"Spoken like a true skeptic. You go around spouting bullshit like you're some kind of psychic philosophical savant with all your intuition about us not being together for very long. As if you can't have control over how you treat me. Why'd you even bother asking me out in the first place if you weren't looking for a relationship? Why not hit up a hookup app and get your kicks with no strings if that's all you wanted?"

"I wanted to get to know you, Lydia. I'm attracted to you. I care...you're interesting and..."

"And what? You're done getting to know me, and now I'm only good for secret sex when you're in the mood? No possibility of anything more. Ever? All because you're going to study abroad for a year. Twelve months out of a whole lifetime, and that's why you can't try with me."

"It's just...when you touch me, it's like you're latching onto my soul. And sometimes it's so strong I just want to get away from that feeling. It's just too much for me to handle right now."

I was floored by his admission and had to sit down. What I'd eaten of my dinner was rolling in my stomach, and I had to take a few deep breaths to keep from seeing it again.

Jason walked over and sat on the table in front of me. "You alright?"

"No, I'm not," I said, getting up again. "You feel the same intense connection I feel between us, and your gut reaction is to run from it while I want to hang onto it with everything I've got. I don't get it. When you were drunk you said you'd push me away if you started to care too much, and I would literally cut myself in fucking half for just the chance to truly be with you and have you love me back."

I left all my stuff sitting on the table and took off out of the classroom. Halfway down the stairs, I heard Jason following me, but I kept running. He called after me, but I didn't stop. I couldn't stop.

"Lydia! I'm sorry I'm not ready to be caught!"

Then he shouldn't have strung himself out on a hook.

Chapter 23
June 26, 2024

Following my GPS directions, I pull to the end of a long dirt road and see a white two-story farmhouse with a large metal building nearby. Kolton's car is parked out front near another car with sorority stickers on the rear glass. It makes me pause since I didn't peg his sister as a sorority girl. I park beside the cars and grab my phone and keys as I get out of my car. I walk toward the open door at the other end of the building and stop when I hear two raised voices inside, one of them belonging to Kolton and the other one female.

"I don't have anything to say to you or Mason," he says. "I have plenty of other friends."

"Holding the anger isn't good for any of us," the woman says. "I want all of us to be friends again, Kolton. I'm sorry we hurt you, but we had to see what would come out of the attraction between us."

"Enough, Maisy! You could have explored all you wanted *after* ending things with me, but you chose to cheat instead. That's not forgivable! You break up with someone before seeing someone else. How is that so difficult? I loved you and was loyal to you. It would have hurt a hell of a lot less if you'd been honest about your feelings."

"I'm sorry. I'm human and I made a mistake. You're not perfect either, you know."

Yikes. I feel guilty eavesdropping on a private conversation, but I'm afraid to interrupt or move at the risk of them hearing me. I decide to wait until I can make my presence known.

"I never said I was perfect, but I'm not the one in the wrong here," Kolton says. "I think you should leave. I don't know why you even bothered to show up here. You know there's no way in hell I'm going to y'all's wedding."

"I had planned to leave the invitation with your parents," she says. "You should know what's going on. Mason misses you."

"That's not my problem. Now please leave. I have a lot of work to do."

"You work too much, Kolton. You need to get back out there. I hate to think of you brooding and not going out with anyone. I always worried you had some kind of problem since you never wanted to have sex when we were together."

"You should go, Maisy. Who I'm sleeping with is none of your business."

"I doubt you're sleeping with anyone."

A moment of silence hits and I know I can't stand by and let her insult him any longer.

I take a deep breath and walk through the door with a huge smile on my face. "Hey, babe!" I call in a singsong voice. "Sorry it took me so long. Traffic was awful." I can see Maisy out of the corner of my eye as I walk toward Kolton. She can't seem to hide her shocked expression at being interrupted.

My back is turned to Maisy when I mouth to Kolton, "Just go with it."

He looks uncertain for a second and recovers quickly with a smile. "It's fine."

I wink at Kolton before standing on my tiptoes to kiss him. I feel the stress leave his face as he wraps his arms around my waist and pulls me toward him—close enough for me to grab his butt. Kolton inhales sharply at the shock of my touch, but he doesn't break our kiss.

When Maisy clears her throat, I pull away and face her, careful to leave my arm wrapped around Kolton's waist. She's tall and pretty with long, light brown hair that frames her face. Her pink cheeks make it clear I've made her uncomfortable. Mission accomplished.

"Oh, hi! I'm Lydia." I extend my hand.

"Maisy," she mumbles, giving me a weak shake before stepping back.

"Oh, well, I didn't expect to—"

"She was just leaving," Kolton interrupts. "Goodbye, Maisy. I wish you and Mason a lifetime of...well...whatever you want and everything the universe has lined out for you."

"Yeah, I should go." Maisy drops her phone as she tries to slip it into her back pocket and again as she tries to pick it up off the concrete floor. She turns and leaves. A moment later, a car door slams, its engine starts, and then gravel spins and hits the metal workshop with little pings as Maisy drives away.

I still have my arm around Kolton's waist as I look up at him. "You okay?" He nods, but I can tell he's lying by the tension in his jaws. I should know; I say I'm fine when I'm not all the time.

"Thank you for that." He turns and rests his forehead against mine for a second before pulling away. "And grabbing my ass was an unexpected but welcome touch. How much did you hear?"

"I heard enough that I had to think fast to make her stop insulting you. If you want to talk about it, I'm here." Not a lie. I'm good at listening and helping with other people's problems even if I sucked at following good advice about my own in the past.

"We can talk about it later. Let's start working on these first." He gestures toward the rest of the room, which is filled with cabinets.

I look around the room and a quick visual count tells me there are at least twenty-five double sets. "Whoa, that's a lot of wood."

Kolton laughs as he hands me some plastic gloves. "It's not too late to run away."

"I'm already here. Show me what to do."

A couple of hours later, we're in a good pattern of staining. Kolton's playlist is perfect, and I'm fine working and listening to him hum along to the songs. It's quiet between us, but it's a comfortable silence.

Kolton finishes one row of cabinets and sets down his supplies on the workbench. He faces me and takes his gloves off, tossing them in a large trash can. "Let's take a break and get some water," he says.

I put the lid back on the stain and remove my gloves. My legs and arms are stiff after working from the floor for so long, so I stretch as I walk to the trash can. Kolton goes to the far corner of the room and pulls two bottles of water from a beat-up refrigerator. He plops down on a torn leather sofa beside the fridge and holds out a bottle for me.

Taking the water, I turn sideways in my seat so I can see him. The water is ice cold, and it's the best drink I've ever had since I hadn't realized how thirsty I was. Unfortunately, it's so cold I give myself a brain freeze and have to struggle to keep from making a fool of myself as I wait for it to pass.

Kolton reaches out and squeezes my knee. "You good?" he asks. I nod, wiping my eyes. "I should have warned you how cold it was."

"No, I'm okay now. I'll recover from the embarrassment in a moment."

"Speaking of embarrassment...sorry about Maisy. I had no idea she was coming by. She and Mason are getting married and wanted to invite my family to the wedding."

"I gathered that from what I overheard."

"I'm not sure if she wanted to rub it in my face or was wanting more gifts. Who knows."

"I know it must have been hard for you."

"About what she said at the end..."

"You don't have to explain. It's none of my business."

"But I want to." Kolton takes a sip of his water. "I've told you Maisy and I dated for a little under a year, right? Well, for the first few months, things were fine, and then she started pressuring me to have sex with her."

I can't keep a poker face after his revelation.

"I know," he continues. "Shocking that a twenty-something guy was the one holding out, but something didn't feel right to me. I was fine with some stuff, but I didn't want to go all the way with her until I was sure it would be a relationship that would last. She stopped talking about it, and I thought she understood. Evidently, she found what she wanted with Mason and just failed to end things with me first. He was my roommate at the time and my best friend—or so I thought."

"I'm sorry you got hurt."

"Looking back, it was probably for the best. Deep down, I think I knew she didn't love me like I loved her. The only regret I have is wasting so much time thinking about what I could have done differently. I don't wish either of them anything bad; I just don't want them in my life."

"Did you have other girlfriends before her?"

"She was the first serious one. I was too dorky and immature in high school, and then I went on a few dates in college that went nowhere before I met Maisy toward the end of my senior year."

He was sharing a significant and surprising detail about his love life. "Wait...are you?"

Kolton nods. "Yep. I'm twenty-five years old, and I'm a virgin. Feel free to laugh at me now."

"It's not funny." I'm unsure what else to say, but I don't feel like laughing. Kolton looks at me like he's waiting for me to say something else. "So...are you waiting until you're married?"

"Not necessarily," he says. "I guess I was just waiting for it to feel right. The right time with the right person. I'm not ashamed or anything, but does it bother you? I mean...does it change your mind about us possibly dating in the future?"

"No. Of course not. It doesn't bother me. I've only been with one person, and sometimes I wish I hadn't, considering all the heartache he caused me." Another truth. Damn, I'm on a roll tonight.

Kolton takes my hand and holds it for a moment. "I'm really glad we met, Lydia," he says, standing and pulling me up with him. "Thanks again for helping me tonight. Both ways." He looks at the unfinished cabinets and groans before turning back to me.

I smile. "I guess we better get back to it."

"Yep. Work waits for no one."

Another couple of hours pass, and we're done with the cabinets. I sit on the sofa again and glance at my phone. It's past eleven o'clock, and I'm exhausted, but in a good way.

Kolton drops onto the sofa beside me and stretches out his long legs, resting his arms across his face. "Thank you so much," he mumbles, not moving his arms. "It's such a relief to have it all done."

"You're welcome." I stretch my arms over my head and then let them fall beside me. My muscles jiggle like Jell-O.

He drops his arms accidentally bumping my shoulder.

I turn toward Kolton and when he looks at me, he snickers. "What?"

"You've got a smudge of stain on your cheek." He gestures, but I'm not sure which side he means.

I try to get it, but I know I didn't based on Kolton's expression. He gets up and wets a paper towel in the sink beside the fridge. He brings it back over and gently scrubs my cheek. He frowns as he pulls the towel away. "It's not coming off," he says, handing the damp towel to me.

"Great."

"Hold on. Let me grab some paint thinner. It'll come off with that."

Kolton gets up and goes to a cabinet on the other side of the room. He comes back with a bottle of paint thinner and takes the towel back from me. He puts a small amount on the towel and uses it to wipe my cheek.

"That did it," he says. "Hold on." He gets up and tosses the towel into the trash before grabbing more off the roll and wetting one in the sink. He comes back and wipes my face, following up with a dry towel. He wads up both towels and tosses them at the trash can, missing it by several feet. Sighing and shaking his head, he turns back to me, cups my chin, and caresses my cheek with his thumb. "It's a little red, but I don't think it hurt your skin."

"Thanks."

He doesn't move his hand and I place mine over his. We lock eyes and I can't look away. His pupils are dilated so much I can barely see the chocolate brown of his irises as we sit in the dimmest section of the building. His friendly and inviting lips display just the hint of a smile, and we're so close I can feel his breath on my face.

I don't know how long we stare at each other, but when Kolton's other hand falls to rest on my thigh, I want to jump out of my skin. He inches closer, and I close the distance between us and kiss him with everything I have. He takes a deep breath through his nose and wraps his arms around me, pulling me into his lap as he deepens our kiss.

It's been a long time since I've wanted anyone so badly—and it worries the hell out of me to acknowledge how starved for affection I've been. My heart feels like I'm being unfaithful to Jason even though my brain keeps reminding me I'm not. But still, I don't break our connection, and neither does Kolton...until a boisterous voice echoes in the building.

"Great job on the cabinets, son!"

We jump and pull away from each other.

An older version of Kolton walks toward us. "Oh! Sorry for interrupting," he says with a chuckle while covering his eyes.

Kolton stumbles out of his seat, and I stand up with him, my face burning like I'm a teenager caught in a compromising position. "Dad! Yeah, we just finished up."

"Looks like it." The man laughs again and extends his hand. "Hi there, young lady. My son seems to have forgotten his manners. George Black."

"Dad, this is my friend Lydia, from the acting workshop."

"Hi," I say, shaking his hand. "Nice to meet you."

"That's not how I pass the time with my friends," George mumbles, nudging his son's shoulder.

Kolton clears his throat, and I know it's time for me to go home.

"I'm heading out. See you tomorrow, Kolton." I walk to the workbench near the door and grab my keys before heading out into the darkness.

Gravel crunches behind me as Kolton jogs to catch up. I turn around and he steps forward awkwardly before embracing me in a hug so warm it feels like home.

"Goodbye," he murmurs, his lips brushing against my forehead. "Text me so I know you've gotten home okay." I hug him back and don't want to let go.

"I will." I close my eyes and think my heart might stop. Something about forehead kisses make them more intimate to me than any others. I imagine letting Kolton be part of my life. In all truth—he already is.

Chapter 24
December 12, 2019

I somehow managed to get through my first semester and pass my finals all while my heart was shattered. Marienne and Vicki tried to comfort me and distract me, but nothing helped fill the void Jason had left in my life. I still saw him at Art Club meetings, and it was excruciating. He was still his ironic self, though he looked a little worse for wear dressed in wrinkled flannel shirts with stubble on his face, like a cross between a 1990s grunge music god and a lumberjack.

The thought of going back home to my parents' house sounded about as appealing as staying in the dorms alone to wallow in self-pity, but I didn't have a choice. The dorms were closing, and all students had to be out the day after their last final. It was midday on a Thursday when it was my turn to leave. Marienne and Vicki had already moved out the evening before after we'd skipped the cafeteria in favor of sharing a final meal of pizza we'd had delivered.

Before she left, Marienne hugged me tightly and made me promise not to call Jason since he didn't deserve to hear from me. She wasn't even speaking to him. I made the vow, but I never would've predicted he'd show up outside my window while I was packing the last of my things.

I knew the moment I heard the tapping on the window, and the heat drained from my whole body as I walked over to open the blinds. In gestures, Jason begged me to open the window. It was cold out, and he wasn't dressed for the weather in a thin denim jacket.

Reluctantly, I unlocked and opened the window as he removed the screen and I found myself standing face-to-face with him for the first time in several weeks. I wanted to touch him more than I wanted to breathe, but I didn't. I couldn't speak at all as I looked into his eyes; I just stood there and crossed my arms, blocking his way in.

"Can I come in and talk to you?" he finally asked after realizing I wasn't going to speak first. I moved to the side and let him in. He crawled through and then closed the window behind him, shivering and rubbing his arms. "It's colder out there than I thought."

He walked toward me, but I took a step back. "What do you want, Jason?"

"I wanted to catch you before you left. Your car was still in the lot, and Marienne let it slip you'd be leaving today."

"Catch me for what? I thought you wanted nothing to do with me. There's nothing left to say."

"I wanted to say goodbye. I'm leaving for Europe right after the new year."

"I know. You could have sent me a text. I thought you were done with me." My eyes filled with tears, and I cursed them as I turned away from him. I felt him walk behind me.

"Lydia," he whispered, wrapping his arms around me. I tried to pull away, but he turned me around and held me, letting me cry. "Please don't cry."

"I can't help it," I mumbled into his chest. "I miss you so much already."

"I'm right here."

I looked up, and then he was kissing me. I knew it was a mistake, but I was suffocating, and he had the only oxygen in the room.

After we'd exhausted ourselves with the best sex we'd ever had, I started to panic and feel nauseated. Nothing had changed, and I knew it deep in my heart. I loved him, and he was still leaving for a year with no promise to come back to me.

"I should get going," Jason said as he walked toward the window. "I'm glad we got to say goodbye. I hope you have a great new year. I want you to be happy, Lydia."

"How do you expect me to be happy when you're leaving?" My voice caught in my throat. "Will I ever hear from you again?"

He stopped with his hands on the windowsill. "I'll be really busy with classes and art projects. I don't think I'll have a lot of free time."

"I'm not asking for much, Jason. Just a call or a text or even an email every now and then will do."

"It's best for you to move on."

"Friends contact each other. You do still want to be friends with me, don't you?"

"It seems like it would be harder on you, and I'm not sure we'd ever work out." Jason turned around to face me. "You want a fairytale romance, and you deserve it, but I don't think I can live up to that. I don't want you to hold yourself back waiting for me when someone else might be what you need right now."

"The only way I'd be holding myself back would be to pretend someone else could fill the gap you're leaving in my heart. It's you I want, Jason. Not some damn fairytale. You're real, and you're flawed, and I love you. I'll be here when you get back."

He sighed and looked at his feet. "I'm the type of person who'll run if you chase me."

"Don't run and I won't have to." My jaw ached as I walked over and wrapped my arms around his waist. "It's killing me you're leaving after we just made love. I'll miss you. Please be careful over there."

He hugged me back tighter than he ever had and kissed my forehead right before pulling back. That was when I noticed a single tear on his cheek. He quickly wiped it away and then climbed out the window, leaving me a shattered mess in his wake.

I drove home to my parents' house crying most of the way and was relieved to find no one home when I got there. I left my bags in the car and let myself in. I let Roscoe follow me to my bedroom and get into bed with me where I pulled the covers over my head. I wanted to go to sleep and wake up in a year when Jason would be back in Arkansas again. But I didn't know then what contagion was lurking in the air just waiting to take hold of the world and the lives of everyone in it.

Chapter 25
July 2, 2024

Though Kolton and I have texted and hung out for meals with our friends from the workshop, we haven't discussed the kiss his father interrupted. I can't stop thinking about it, though. He's the only guy besides Jason I've kissed because I wanted to and not as part of a play or acting exercise. It means my heart is moving on as much as it terrifies me.

I don't feel awkward around Kolton, and he's just as kind as ever. I have to admit I'd like to kiss him again and hope he still feels the same, but more than anything, I don't want to fall in love again if it'll mean getting my heart broken. What if I'm not strong enough to deal with new emotions? And what if I am ready? Does it mean I'm finally getting over Jason?

When Kolton nudges me, I realize I've zoned out on the last of Bernetta's announcements for us. The other actors are gathering their things and saying goodbye for our long break. In addition to our regular Wednesday off, we have Thursday and Friday off to celebrate Independence Day.

"You were somewhere else for a moment," he says after everyone except Bernetta has left. She's still stuffing papers into her tote bag in the corner. "You good?"

I shake to clear my head and don't feel the need to lie. "Not really. Just a lot on my mind, I guess."

"I hope I'm not adding to your stress."

Bernetta walks over to us. "I'm impressed. In the exercise today, you had me convinced of sexual tension between you two. Excellent acting without being over the top. Keep up the great work." She pats each of us on the shoulder. "Now let's get outta here and enjoy the holiday break."

We follow her and watch her lock the doors. She gets into her car and waves to us as she drives away. Everyone else has already left, leaving the parking lot deserted. Kolton's car is parked beside mine, so we walk over together. He looks at his feet and shuffles them a bit, then rubs the back of his neck. It's cute seeing him nervous. It's the first time we've been alone since our intense kiss that might have progressed to a full make-out session.

"So..." I say.

He chuckles and looks up. "I'm really bad at this," he says with a sigh. "Wanna grab some dinner with me?"

"I'd love to."

"Great."

"So where should we go?"

Kolton laughs again. "I hadn't thought that far ahead. I wasn't sure if you'd want to go."

"I'm not in the mood to go somewhere loud, but a quiet place would be nice."

He looks over my head toward his car. "What if we just grab a pizza and go to my place?"

My heart jumps into my throat. I have a brief flashback to Jason's tendencies to keep us secret, but I push down the feelings. Kolton is not Jason. "Okay, how far away are you?"

"Less than five miles." He points to his car. "Just ride with me and I'll bring you back here later. I think your car'll be fine."

Kolton gets a pepperoni pizza (my favorite) from Little Caesars, and then we're at his place in no time. The building is cute and has a gated entrance. I follow him up the stairs to the tiny apartment on the third floor. He lets us in then locks and chains the door behind us. He puts the pizza box down on the trunk he's using as a coffee table and invites me to sit on his torn black leather sofa.

When Does Life Begin?

I sit and look around the room as Kolton goes into the kitchen for drinks. There's an Aztec-printed area rug trying and failing to cover the stained beige carpet and a large flat-screen TV mounted to the opposite wall. There are a few play posters on the wall but not much more in terms of décor. I see a fleece blanket draped over a recliner in the back corner next to the window and a reading lamp. There's a small bookshelf beside it. Behind me is a door that must lead to his bedroom and bathroom.

Kolton sticks his head out the passthrough to the kitchen and asks me if water is okay before returning with two glasses, two plates, and a roll of paper towels. He sits beside me and then closes his eyes for a moment before opening the pizza box to serve me a slice.

"What was that?" I ask. "A prayer or something?"

Kolton nods as he takes his own slice. "I never lost the habit," he says. "It's good to be thankful."

"I get it."

"Do you want to talk about what had you so distracted at the end of class today?" he asks between bites. "I hope I didn't make you uncomfortable during our exercise."

I take another bite to give myself time to answer and know the truth is best. "I think we both know there was no acting going on between us today, Kolton. It took everything in my distracted mind to not keep going and just kiss you before Bernetta yelled 'cut.'"

He starts coughing and has to take a drink before he can respond. "Ten points for honesty."

"Are you okay?"

"Yep." He clears his throat. "So, what do we do? We've both been through some shit, and I meant what I said about not pressuring you."

171

"There aren't any rules against dating in the workshop agreement, and we like each other. We should just go for it, right?"

"I think so."

After he's finished eating, Kolton puts his plate on the trunk. I do the same with mine and turn toward him on the sofa, pulling one leg underneath me. He has pizza sauce on his chin, and I can't resist reaching up to wipe it away with my thumb. When he takes my hand and licks away the sauce, I almost fall out of my seat, but he keeps me upright. My whole body comes alive again since it's the first time I've wanted to have sex with someone other than Jason, even though I know it's too soon for us. And it's taking a giant leap Kolton even wants to go there with me and have me be his first.

"You look like a deer caught in the headlights," Kolton says, squeezing my hand. "You sure you're good with us dating?"

I lean forward and let my head rest on his shoulder to hide my reddening face. "Of course, I'm fine. Terrified, but fine."

"I don't mean to scare you," he says, leaning his head against mine.

"It's the feelings I'm having that...well, you know it's been a long time since I've felt this way for someone. I'm happy about it, but I'm also scared of getting hurt again."

"I'm glad you feel comfortable being honest with me."

"I've lied a lot in the past, mostly to myself, and did a whole lot of pretending to be okay when I wasn't. Earlier, I panicked when you suggested we come to your apartment rather than go out. I thought you maybe didn't want to be seen with me, even though we've eaten at the diner together before. I realize it's trauma from my last relationship and has nothing to do with you or us, but I get some pretty irrational thoughts sometimes."

Kolton takes my hands. "Lydia, I wouldn't want to keep our relationship a secret. I think you're amazing, and I'll send a group text right now to everyone in the workshop to tell them we're dating if you want me to."

"That's not necessary," I say, looking down at our intertwined hands. "You're not responsible for curing all my neurotic fears."

"I don't want to add to them." Kolton leans closer and speaks softly. "I promise I'll be careful with your heart if you'll do the same with mine."

I look up to meet his eyes as mine fill with tears. I can't speak, so I just nod and try to wipe my eyes, but Kolton stops me and pulls me into a hug. That's all it takes for the floodgates to open, and I start sobbing, unable to stop for a couple of minutes. I'd probably die from humiliation if Kolton wasn't holding me and whispering in my ear that everything will be okay.

Strangely, I feel better than I have in months once I get my emotions under control. I'm still lying in Kolton's arms on his couch and he's gently rubbing my shoulder. We haven't spoken for several minutes, and I'm not sure I want to get up, but I know I have to go home at some point to avoid freaking out my mom.

"So...I'm embarrassed," I say as I pull myself from Kolton's embrace. "I didn't mean to get so emotional."

"It's okay," he says. "You've been through a lot, and sometimes it just comes to a head. I get it."

"I guess."

"Hey," he says, cupping my chin. "Just to be clear, I want to date you exclusively. I'm not comfortable seeing different people at the same time."

"I feel the same."

"Good. I'm glad we agree." He stands and takes my hands to pull me up. "I know you probably want to head home, so I'll take you back to your car."

"You're right, I need to go home."

The ride back to my car is calm as we listen to music and chat about the upcoming holiday. Kolton invites me to spend the Fourth with him and his family on Thursday, but I'm not even sure yet what my family has planned, so I'll let him know tomorrow.

Once we're back in the parking lot, he gets out to walk me to my car. I appreciate the gesture and definitely appreciate the goodnight kiss. I know I shouldn't compare kisses between Kolton and Jason, but Kolton is better at it.

From the time Jason had left my dorm back in December, I'd just been going through the motions to get through each day. I missed him more than I'd ever missed anyone or anything. It felt like part of my soul was misplaced and the hole grew larger with each passing day.

I hadn't heard from him since he'd sent me a text to let me know he'd arrived safely and would have limited phone access with all the projects and studying. I had his email address too, and I'd poured my heart out to him at least once a week to remind him I was still there for him.

Marienne hadn't heard from her cousin either. She was deep in preparation for the role of Blanche in our theatre department's upcoming spring production of A Streetcar Named Desire. I'd won the role of Stella and read through my lines day and night in addition to the scheduled rehearsals.

Vicki did everything in her power to keep me busy with shopping and mini road trips to take my mind off things, but nothing worked. When the fun was over, I still felt sad and out of place, but I carried on.

By mid-March, there was talk on the news about a virus called COVID-19 making its way to the United States and we were sent home for two weeks to lessen the curve according to the government. I worried about Jason being stranded overseas, and I was thrilled when he finally emailed me back to say that his program was continuing with modifications, social distancing, and mandatory masks. I wrote back that I loved him and wanted him to be careful.

The brief change to online-only classes soon became the plan for the rest of the semester. We modified our play into a radio theatre production recorded live over the internet and archived for playbacks. I was isolated from everyone except my parents despite meeting online and talking on the phone.

I handled grocery shopping for Grammy and dropped things off on her front porch. We visited through her screen door with me wearing a mask and standing out on her sidewalk to be safe. I longed to hug her, but I didn't want to risk her life in case I'd been exposed somehow. Despite all our precautions, she caught the virus in July—we think from the gentleman who came to fix her air conditioner. We'd never know for sure.

Outfitting myself with two masks and enough hand sanitizer to supply my whole family, I moved in with Grammy to nurse her back to health. At first, she seemed to improve, but then her fever came back even higher, and she struggled to breathe.

Grammy insisted she just needed a few more days to rest, but I had a bad feeling about the whole situation. The last time I saw her was when the paramedics loaded her into the ambulance in her driveway. I'd known then she wouldn't make it through and suspected she'd developed pneumonia. She'd been too weak to speak and died in the hospital a week later.

My heart was broken in a new way at the thought of Grammy dying alone, but protocols prevented visitors from going in. A kind nurse had put me on speakerphone to say my goodbyes and stayed with her until the end. We held an outdoor and socially distant funeral to lay her to rest in mid-July on an unusually cool morning. Her masked bridge club friends were all there, displaying more stoicism than I could, each of them looking frailer than I'd ever noticed.

After I got home from Grammy's funeral, I emailed Jason again. I didn't expect a reply since I hadn't heard from him since March.

Dear Jason,

I know you're busy with the program, but I really need you to reply to me just this once, so I'll know you're okay. My grandma, who was my absolute favorite person in the whole world, died last week of COVID. She was always such a force and so strong. I still can't believe she's gone. I feel like I'm too young to be dealing with all this, but I'm her only living relative so I've inherited her house at 19 years old.

I'm planning to sell the place because I can't stand the thought of living there with all the memories associated with it. Maybe it's a mistake, but for now, I feel at peace with the decision. I'm putting the important things in storage and trying to get everything cleaned out before school starts back.

Last semester was pretty much a bust and this coming one will be weird with the mask requirements. I feel like I haven't seen any faces not on a screen except my parents' and stepbrother's in so long. At least I can hide behind my mask of sadness. I know I won't see Grammy again, but I'm counting the days until I'll see you again. I will see you again soon, won't I?
With all my love,
Lydia

I was thrilled to find a message in my inbox later that week. But I soon realized I should've been more careful what I'd wished for.

Lydia,

I'm fine. Just busy. I'm sorry to hear about your grandma. I was close with mine too, so I know what that's like.

I told you not to wait on me. But the way you tell me you love me all the time makes me think you're not trying to date anyone. I know the virus makes things weird, but you should see someone next semester. I don't want you to be lonely. I've been seeing someone here for the last couple of weeks. She's a student in another program. I think you'd like her.

I know it won't go anywhere in the long run since neither of us want anything permanent right now, but I owed it to myself to explore it since I had a feeling my time with her would be short just like it was with you. I understand you want a forever kind of relationship. I know there's someone out there for you, and he'll be around when you're ready to find him. You deserve someone who can be what you want right now.
Jason

All the tears I'd shed during the past week had done nothing to prepare my body for the shock of learning Jason was seeing someone else. The realization that I'd been pining away for him while he hadn't even been thinking about me shattered my already broken heart.

Devastation clouded over me, and I couldn't get enough air. It didn't matter how much I loved him or felt he was my soulmate; he just didn't want me right now or maybe ever. It'd been better when I hadn't known.

Marienne, Vicki, and I moved back to the dorms for in-person classes in August, though everyone was required to wear masks outside our rooms. Everything felt different. Gone was the excitement and possibility I'd felt freshman year. I was a shell of a person, missing my grandma and still heartbroken over Jason.

Marienne had allowed me the rest of the summer to wallow in self-pity before telling me it was time to move on from a guy who didn't deserve me. She and Vicki dragged me to outdoor parties and every socially-distant campus activity she could find. The distractions helped, but at night, I'd still dream about Jason—often about his death. Sometimes he'd die in my arms, and other times I'd wake up shaking from a nightmare where he'd died alone in a dark space far away from me.

Our fall theatre production of *Our Town* went on as planned in a makeshift outdoor stadium with audience group seating and actors placed six feet apart. Though I'd desperately wanted the role of Emily, seeing Marienne perform it was the next best thing while I played her mother, Mrs. Webb.

The semester was over soon enough, and I hoped for a COVID-19 vaccine while many anti-maskers emerged with convoluted conspiracy theories. Reading about and watching the hate unfold around me was sickening. I would have done just about anything to have my grandma back and hearing about people in the United States who claimed the virus didn't exist made me furious.

After I'd moved back home for the holiday break, Marienne called and mentioned her cousin's name to me for the first time since August. I had to end the call early because I didn't want her to hear me cry.

Jason wasn't coming home. He'd completed his classes online for his bachelor's and was extending his stay for two years to work on his master's degree. Despite everything, I'd still hoped up until that point we'd see each other again when he got back, and things would work out. That he'd see me and realize we belonged together.

It didn't matter how many times I told my stubborn heart to let him go and to be angry with him, I couldn't. I still loved him. I'd known being away from him for a year would be difficult, and the prospect of waiting another two sounded impossible. I pressed pause on my broken heart and tried to find a way to numb it so I could stop missing someone who would never be mine.

I've become more comfortable in Dr. Benson's office over the last few weeks. She barely has her pen poised before I start speaking.

"I know I'm supposed to talk about my dad today, but there's more on my mind than that. About Kolton. I helped him with a project, and we kissed. We talked a lot, and I found out he's a virgin, so I don't think there'll be any pressure for sex even though we've decided to start dating."

Dr. Benson puts down her pen. "That's a big step for you since you've said you didn't think you could date or fall in love again. How are you feeling about your decision to see someone again?"

"Excited and a little scared at the same time. I don't want to get hurt again, and I was honest with Kolton about that. His ex cheated with his best friend, so he's been through hurt too, and feels like taking things slowly. Slow is best for me, I know. But I can't help but feel like I'm cheating on Jason."

"Is that a healthy thought?"

"No. I realize things with Jason ended a long time ago. And if I'm honest with myself, he and I were never together the way I wanted us to be. He may have been my boyfriend, but I was never his girlfriend. There's nothing I can do about the way things ended between us and as much as I'll always love him, I can't let it stop me from living my life. He and I just weren't meant to be together no matter how much I wanted it or thought it would eventually happen."

"It sounds like you've been doing a lot of thinking."

"Yeah. That, and I've been talking to him. To Jason, I mean."

I notice the shock on my doctor's face before she can hide it. She clears her throat and makes a note in her book. "Why don't you tell me about that?"

"I told you about going to the cemetery for the first time since the funeral last month and how I sat on a bench near Marienne's grave."

Dr. Benson nods and continues writing.

"Well, it's become an almost weekly thing since then, and that's where I've been talking to Jason. I'm trying to work through some feelings from our relationship and everything with the accident. It's almost like we have a standing appointment."

"I see," she says. "A lot of people find comfort in visiting cemeteries where loved ones are buried. Do you ever talk to Marienne? Or to your dad."

"I have, and I know both of them would want me to be happy. I also know I can't keep talking to Jason. It isn't good for me to prolong the pain. He'll have to stay in my past since he can't be part of my life anymore. I can't keep letting the memories and the dreams hurt me. And if it means stopping my visits to the cemetery, I think Marienne would understand. It's just..." I only thought I was getting good at not crying in Dr. Benson's office; it's starting all over again.

She stops writing and hands me a box of tissues. "Just what?"

"It still hurts so much and I'm not ready to say goodbye even though it's already over. My relationship with him was a slow death from the beginning, I just didn't know it then. And even when we got back together for a while after he finally came home from Europe, I was terrified the whole time he'd leave me again and..." I crumple a tissue and think about my mother. It must be how she feels about me every day since I got home from the hospital after attempting suicide. The ache in my heart shifts and I'm overwhelmed with grief for what I've done to her, my family, and my friends.

"You stopped talking. Do you want to share some more of what's on your mind?"

"I'm trying to come to terms with how selfish I've been since the accident. I know I wasn't the only person hurting, and I hurt a lot of people when I tried to end my own pain. My mom, my stepdad, my stepbrother, my friends. And I know my dad and grandparents would have been disappointed in me too. Marienne especially since she was so full of life the brief time I knew her."

"Suicide is an inherently selfish decision, Lydia, but when someone makes that decision, I truly believe they're not able to think logically, barring some terminal illness, of course. You experienced a great shock and fell into a deep depression. The accident robbed you of closure and getting to say goodbye. It's possible it brought up some repressed feelings about your father, whose sudden death traumatized you before you were truly old enough to process and understand the profound loss."

"I grew up feeling like something was missing with my dad being gone, but I also had Larry, who always treated me like his daughter and still does. I remember him holding me and crying after I woke up in the psych ward. Is it bad I still don't remember exactly what I did that day, only what I've been told about it?"

"A lot of people block out trauma or parts of it. And we agreed when I started seeing you last year we'd wait and talk about some of it when you were ready. Are you ready to make any statements to that effect yet?"

I know exactly what I need to say—something I know in my heart. I can't though. Not yet. Saying it means I have to acknowledge and let go of feelings when I'm not sure I know how or what will become of me without them.

Shaking my head, I close my eyes. "No. Not yet. I can't say it."

"What *can* you say?"

"I'm not okay yet."

"And?"

"It's okay I'm not there yet. I've lost my grandparents, my dad, and one of my best friends. I've lost love. My heart is broken and as it's healing, the scars are causing more pain, but I'm strong enough to get through it this time. I have to be strong enough. I will be. I am strong."

"Let's talk a little about your dad. Do you think your life would be different now if your dad were still alive?"

"Probably. How could it not be? I mean, I love Larry and Luke and can't imagine my life without them, but what if? Larry's been a great dad as I'm sure my dad would've been. And who's to say I wouldn't have had other siblings, or my parents wouldn't have split up later on? Maybe I'm just messed up, period, and it has nothing to do with losing my father at such a young age—or maybe it has everything to do with who I am and why I feel the need to hide my true emotions behind stage personas so much."

"So, acting gives you permission to feel your feelings without having to own them?"

"I guess so. Maybe that's what drew me to acting in the first place. I started auditioning for school plays as soon as I could. It was comforting to be someone else."

"I think you should try journaling or writing a letter to yourself. Perhaps work on a play and give yourself a part to help you work through all these feelings. What do you think?"

I sigh as I stand up, exhausted from our session. "I'll try it."

It's late afternoon, and I spent most of the morning after my appointment trying to talk myself out of driving to the cemetery, but yet here I am again. I'm not sure anymore if I come here to punish myself or work on healing—maybe both. Either way, I have a handwritten letter in my pocket—a goodbye note for Jason.

He's already sitting on the bench when I arrive, and I don't speak as I settle in beside him. I lean down to straighten the artificial flowers from my last two visits. When I turn to look at Jason's profile, his eyes are unfocused like he's deep in thought. He can join the club because thinking's all I've done since leaving Dr. Benson's office.

When Jason finally speaks, the sound startles me. "Why do you keep coming here, Lydia?"

"I'm still working that out," I say. "But probably the guilt of feeling like the accident was my fault since Marienne was driving to see me. At least that's my therapist's opinion. She also thinks I may be hanging on so tightly to the feelings I have or had for you because I don't like to be wrong or confused about things. Perfectionism at its finest.

"So, I'm either the biggest idiot or the biggest liar who doesn't have a clue how she really feels since I still wake up every damn day telling myself I loved you—that I always will in some way. Even while I think I'm moving on. No, I am moving on, damn it. I have to. I'm tired of being lonely and beating myself up for feeling like I wasn't good enough for you."

"Everything you say screams 'conflicted,' but I sense you're less so now. I hope you'll believe it yourself soon. I've always seen greatness in you."

"It's funny—I always believed in you but struggled to believe in myself. And with you, it was the opposite. You believed in me, but you never believed in yourself or wanted me the way I wanted you. I understand now we were never meant to be, Jason, but why, why did it have to hurt so bad to love you?"

"I didn't have an answer."

"I would have sold my soul to get you to love me, but even when you came back from Europe and we started messing around again, deep down, I knew it was wrong. I knew you'd leave me again, and I loved you too much for you to ever be mine for real."

"Love isn't always enough."

My eyes sting, and I clutch my chest. "It's still so raw, and I want it to stop hurting so I can let myself be with somebody else. He's a good guy, and I'm terrified of him hurting me like you did, but I owe it to him and to myself to try because I can't live like this anymore."

"I'm glad there's someone else now. You should be open to possibilities."

"His name is Kolton, and when we kiss, I feel it everywhere, just like I did with you at first—until I started to feel a dull ache every time our lips parted. And it scares the hell out of me. I've kissed several people while acting, Jason, and they all felt the same—as casual as bumping into someone in a crowded hallway.

"But no one else has ever felt like you. Or like Kolton. I'm afraid to let myself fall in love again because I honestly don't know if I can stand it. And if I'm being honest, whoever I end up with forever—if that even happens—will have to love me more than I love him because I need to keep at least one foot on the ground at all times or I'll risk floating away like I did with you. I can't lose myself again. Not when I'm just now learning to love my flaws and scars and pain and everything."

Jason nods, but he doesn't speak.

"My therapist suggested I write a letter to myself, but all I wanted was to write a letter to you, so I did and I'm going to read it now."

Dear Jason,

Five years ago, you met a young and vulnerable girl who fell in love with you. I gave you everything special about myself all wrapped up in a heart-shaped box, hoping you'd feel the same. Every star in the sky shined brighter when I was with you until the pain of the discarded box grew into bitterness.

When you returned the box, it was torn and tattered but still repairable because you'd left behind an impression that worked like glue, pliable and able to mold into a resemblance of what was there before.

Hope kept me going until you returned and destroyed what was left of my pieced-together heart. No longer feeling strong enough to keep going without you, I faltered before finding the strength to rise again.

I'll love you always and know now that what we had wasn't meant to last forever. But it has left a lasting impression on my heart. I can only hope I left some sort of impression on you even if you could never love me. You hurt me more than I will ever allow anyone else to, and with that, I'll lock away the broken box in my heart one last time and seal it away for safekeeping. I'm finally ready to let you go.

Goodbye,

Lydia

I close my eyes to stop the flow of tears and feel Jason's arms wrap around me. It's not lustful or a touch that repels me, but it feels final for the first time—a touch so complete it envelopes me in coldness and warmth simultaneously. The goodbye I think I've always needed to truly let him go.

"I'm sorry for everything," he says into my ear in a voice barely louder than a whisper.

"I'm sorry too."

When he releases me, I open my eyes again and take a deep breath. "I forgive you, Jason." He nods, urging me to continue "But most of all, I forgive myself. This is it. I can't see you anymore. I can't if I want to heal, and I do."

"Goodbye, Lydia. I wish you happiness and truth in everything you'll accomplish."

"Goodbye, Jason."

Back in my car, I'm not sure what to do with myself. I don't have to work until Friday evening, and I don't want to go home either so I use my car's Bluetooth connection to text Kolton and ask if I can stop by. It doesn't take him long to text back that he wants to see me. At least I have a destination now.

Chapter 28
January 4, 2023

I felt like I was dying, but I didn't want to dwell on it. Almost three years had passed since the virus hit the States. I'd been vaccinated and managed to avoid it even while working at a dollar store after the mask mandates were lifted. Not anymore. The little pink lines on the at-home COVID-19 test were mocking me, and I felt like death zombified.

Marienne was still at home visiting her parents and working until classes started again. I'd come back early from visiting mine to work and to spend some time alone with my thoughts in the apartment we'd shared off campus since the beginning of our senior year.

During the past week, I'd only been to work and one other place to pick up a grocery order, so I figured I'd caught the virus from a customer. I called Marienne and let her know to stay away until I was well and could sanitize our place. She wanted to come back early to take care of me, but I declined. Same conversation with my mother right after that. I didn't want them to get sick, and I was young and strong. I could handle COVID. It was highly unlikely I'd die from it like my grandmother.

When I'd finally seen Marienne again at the start of the fall semester after Jason had dropped the bombshell during quarantine, she'd hugged me tightly and promised me my heart would heal. And it had to a point. There was no choice but to go on. At least no one could see I wasn't smiling all the time behind my mask.

And when Marienne revealed Jason had completed his degree requirements online and had decided to stay in Europe indefinitely, I might have relapsed a bit, but I persevered and powered through as the mask requirements were lifted and we were back to semi-normal at the university.

After that, my friends and I had a pact to not discuss Jason again, although it hadn't stopped me from thinking about him, missing him, and dreaming about him almost every night.

But things had gotten better. My sophomore and junior years were filled with classes, theatre productions, and tons of laughing with Marienne and Vicki at school and with Phoebe during the summers we spent at home working. I'd kissed three different guys during plays and hadn't felt anything—not so much as a brief tingle—even though two of them had asked me out when our respective productions were over. Both guys were funny and kind, but neither could take hold of my heart, which was still broken.

My fever finally broke five days after the positive test, and for the first time that week, I was able to stand while I showered rather than sit on the tiled floor and cry while I washed my hair and let the lather run over the rest of me. Marienne, Vicki, Phoebe, and my mom had checked in on me every day, and Luke had called twice via FaceTime so he could get a look at me.

After a couple of days with no fever, I started to feel more human and set out to sanitize our apartment, making sure to clean every surface with disinfectant and open all the windows to air out any remaining germs despite the cold temperature.

I didn't need to go anywhere since I hadn't eaten all the groceries I'd bought right before getting sick. I'd mostly survived on the sports and protein drinks Marienne had left on our doorstep since the last thing I'd wanted to do was cook. I still didn't feel like cooking, so I ordered something through Bite

Squad and sat down on our old sofa to rest after the cleaning marathon.

Almost an hour later, my doorbell rang, and I jumped up and opened the door without checking, expecting to find a delivery driver with my food. And that's what I found, but the identity of the driver nearly stopped my heart.

His hair was long again in braided pigtails that hung behind his shoulders and the same scruffy goatee accented his thin lips that were twisted into a slight smirk. And the clear blue eyes I'd dreamt of so many times during the past three years were now burning a hole through my soul again. I had to grab the doorframe to steady myself as he spoke.

"I have your order from A Hole in the Wall, Lydia." Jason held out the bag to me.

"Thanks," I said, taking the bag. We stood in awkward silence for an excruciatingly long time before I couldn't take it anymore and stepped back inside, closing the door behind me. I dropped the bag on the floor and fell to my knees beside the door, leaning my head against it. Breathing was a struggle and more difficult than I remembered. Then knocking on the door startled me back to my senses.

"Lydia! I wanna talk to you. Please, will you hear me out?"

Despite everything, it didn't take me more than a fraction of a second to decide to let him in. Not even bothering to get up completely, I rose to my knees and opened the door. If Jason was surprised to find me kneeling, he didn't acknowledge it. He stepped inside and watched me as I closed the door and sat down with my back to it. He looked at the sofa and back down at me before he settled on the floor in front of the coffee table.

"You okay?" he asked. "You seem—"

"I'm fine. I was sick last week with COVID, but I'm better now." Lies. All lies. I was as far away from fine as possible, torn between wanting to throw something at him or throw myself on top of him. My entire love life hinged on what he might say.

Jason pointed to the discarded bag of food on the floor. "You should eat before it gets cold."

Eating was the last thing I wanted to do, especially with my heart stuck in my throat. I got up long enough to grab the bag and take it to the kitchen where I tossed it in the fridge. When I turned back to the small living room, Jason was sitting on the sofa. I took a spot in the ugly orange recliner Marienne's dad had given us and stared at Jason.

"Not hungry anymore?"

I covered my eyes with my arms and let my head fall back on the chair. "Why are you here?"

"I'm working Bite Squad to make ends meet before the semester starts. I'll be teaching adjunct a couple of art classes, and it doesn't pay much. I don't want to live with my parents forever."

"And?"

"I saw your name pop up for an order in my area and thought I'd grab it so I could come by and see you."

"Cut the bullshit, Jason. I haven't heard from you in forever, then you just showed up on my doorstep."

"Didn't Marienne tell you I came home at Christmas last month?"

"Obviously not. We don't talk about you. And you made it pretty clear you didn't want anything to do with me after you went to Europe, got a girlfriend after saying you weren't interested in having one, and then didn't come back. Or maybe it was you didn't want me. But whatever it was, it's over, and it's been over for a long time." But it wasn't over for me, and I doubted it ever would be. Just having him in the same room made me feel alive again, and it wasn't from getting over being sick.

Jason sighed and moved closer to me. "I didn't go to Europe and get a girlfriend. Michelle and I were only seeing each other casually until she left, and I stayed. It wasn't serious—we were both homesick when we met and only hung out a couple of months. Later, with everything still going on with the virus, I just wasn't ready to come home and face reality."

"You surely didn't want to face me. And whatever you did with her over there was serious enough to hurt me. I wish you hadn't told me at all; I didn't want to know her name."

"You'd rather me lie to you? I told you when we first went out, I wasn't ready for something serious. I never wanted to hurt you."

"That's not the point. I was in love with you. I told you before we started having sex, before you said you wanted to keep seeing me. And you knew how I felt before you left, whether you believed it or not, and you started something with me again that night anyway. For what reason, I don't know but I'm an idiot for letting it—"

"Because when I'm around you, I'm drawn to you like a magnet. I knew I'd miss you while I was gone, and I wanted a good memory. I tried to stay away from you before so I wouldn't hurt you. I didn't know I'd be gone so long, or I'd be so lonely over there."

"Lonely? You chose to extend your stay another two years. And you missed me? I missed you too, and you only reached out after my grandma died. I'd written to you plenty of times before and heard nothing before you dropped that bomb on me. Did you even care how I felt, Jason?"

"It doesn't mean I didn't care; I just didn't know what to say. I wanted you to be happy while I was gone, and I thought if you would see someone else it might help." He twisted the ends of his hair around his fingers as he looked at me.

"I find it hard to believe you cared about me or missed me at all since it wasn't enough to keep you from screwing around with someone else. Me missing you couldn't have been solved by going out with another guy. And I don't believe you didn't have five spare minutes to text me or email me once in a while. It's called 'communication' and you suck at it."

"I know. I did everything wrong, but I'm hoping we can start over and at least be friends again."

"I'm not sure we were ever friends, Jason, or if it's even possible now after everything."

He looked down at his hands. "Do you still love me?"

"If you have to ask me then you really are dumber than I thought."

Jason cracked a smile and stood up, but I stayed seated. "I should let you rest. I'm glad you're starting to feel better. I caught COVID after I took a trip to Amsterdam last year and it was rough." He walked toward the door and put his hand on the knob.

"I worried about you every day after the virus broke out. So many people were dying, and I thought I might never see you again."

He turned around and leaned against the door. "I was careful as I could be, but I should have done better about reaching out to you or Marienne. She's not my biggest fan at the moment. She gut-punched me when I tried to hug her after I got home."

"She hasn't said a word about you since she told me about your master's program." It wasn't entirely true. She'd mentioned him a couple of times since then but only using terms of endearment like "dickhead cousin" or "shit-for-brains cousin." I wasn't sorry she'd hit him though, and I hoped it had hurt. I'm sure it was for more reasons than just what he'd done to me.

"You look good, Lydia. I like your hair longer like that."

I picked at the ends of my hair, which had grown out to reach the middle of my back. "I've been thinking about cutting it shorter again, but I haven't decided."

"You're beautiful either way."

I couldn't respond.

"Anyway, I should go pick up a few more orders for the night." He opened the door and stepped out before turning around again. "Can I text you or call you later tonight?"

I got up so I could lock the door behind him and stopped on the threshold. "Not tonight. I'm going back to work in the morning and need to rest. But maybe tomorrow night."

Jason backed away. "I hope you don't think I was just using you for sex back then. I cared about you. I still do." He turned and left without giving me a chance to respond, but I couldn't have spoken anyway. And damn it if my eyes hadn't betrayed me and filled with tears.

The woman who opens Kolten's door after I knock is someone I haven't met, but one look at her makes their relationship clear. Kendra is nearly as tall as her brother and has the same light hair and warm brown eyes.

As she grins at me, the small stud in her nose sparkles, "At last we meet," she says, pulling me into a hug. "At least, I hope you're Lydia. If not, my brother has some explaining to do. He's told me so much about you over the last month, I feel like we should be friends by now."

"Nice to meet you too, Kendra." I take a step into the apartment after she releases me and notice several open Chinese take-out containers sitting on Kolton's makeshift coffee table. I hear the toilet flush through the open bedroom door. "I didn't mean to interrupt your dinner," I say as Kolton walks into the living room.

"You're not!" he says, coming over to give me a quick peck on the lips. It's a very boyfriend-like thing to do, and I'm surprised we're already at that stage.

"Definitely not," Kendra says.

"Are you hungry?" Kolton asks. "I was just about to put away the leftovers."

"No, thank you." It's been an emotional day, and eating's the last thing on my mind.

Kendra drags me away from her brother and over to the couch. "Now, tell me everything you can about yourself before I have to leave. And stick to the juicy stuff since Kolt's told me everything else."

I give Kendra my standard actor's bio while Kolton cleans up the remnants of their dinner, and I genuinely like her. She's refreshing and confident, not caring that she snorts when she laughs. Soon she's telling me stories about their childhood complete with an action-packed impression of Kolton running around with underwear on his head like he did when he was a kid. He's graduated from tighty-whities and superhero undies to neutral boxer briefs based on what Kendra pulled from the laundry basket for her demonstration.

Kendra finds it hilarious that their dad walked in on Kolton and me kissing but says not to worry about it since both of their parents are much more comfortable with heterosexual relationships. It's the only time during our conversation I catch a hint of sadness in her eyes, so I reach out and squeeze her hand before asking her to tell me about her girlfriend.

When Kendra leaves about an hour later, my abs are aching from laughing so hard, and I realize I needed that as much as I needed to see Kolton tonight. As soon as he's closed and locked the door, he comes back to the couch where I'm sitting and stretches out beside me.

"Just couldn't stay away from me, could you?" he teases as he wraps his arms around me and pulls me close for a kiss.

I shiver despite it still being over 90 degrees outside. Every touch from him is electric, and I'm scared to death but more terrified to ignore my feelings. "I'm really nervous," I blurt out.

Kolton takes my hand and places it over his heart, which is pounding. "Me too," he says. "But in a good way. What about you? Your feelings good?"

"Mostly." I grin, knowing I won't lie to him.

He responds with a frown.

"I've had a rough day, but it's much better now. My feelings for you are definitely good."

"Wanna talk about it?"

"Not tonight. I've done a lot of talking about my screwed-up feelings to my therapist today, so I'd rather focus on the ones that aren't."

"Okay, but I'll listen to all your feelings, screwed-up or not."

"I don't want to start bawling on you again. I've cried enough in therapy and at the cemetery."

"Still going every Wednesday, huh?"

"Just about. I went to my dad's and grandparents' graves at a different cemetery on Father's Day. I was closest to my dad's mother, my Grammy Dawson. She died of COVID four years ago."

"I'm so sorry. My dad lost his brother to it. My uncle did a lot of traveling for business and caught it right after some of the travel bans got lifted."

"It's awful. Even with the vaccine and the boosters, I caught it about a year and a half ago."

"Yeah, me too. It was right after Thanksgiving. I just holed up here and suffered through it."

My phone rings from my purse, and I recognize the ringtone as my stepbrother wanting to FaceTime with me. It's been a bit since I've talked to him and he's a couple of days into his residency. I answer it at Kolten's insistence while he goes to the kitchen to get us water.

Luke's pale face fills my screen. "Hey, sis," he says. "How's it going?"

"Not bad," I say. "You look like a zombie, though, Dr. Carmichael. Have you slept at all?"

"I will soon. It's like I'm starting school all over again with this residency. There's so much I don't know."

"You'll be amazing. Those kids are so lucky to have you."

"How are you? Sleeping, therapy, meds?"

Kolton places a glass of water in front of me and sits down.

"Yes, doc, I'm fine."

"Where are you? I don't recognize the place."

"I'm at Kolton's apartment." I turn the phone sideways to let Kolton appear with me on screen. "Luke, this is Kolton Black. Kolton, this is Luke Carmichael." Kolton offers a wave.

"Hey," Luke says.

"Nice to meet you," Kolton says. "Lydia has lots of nice things to say about you."

"Good to meet you too."

"Kolton and I are in the acting workshop together this summer. The director thinks we have a real shot at getting the lead parts."

"That's awesome," Luke says, rubbing his eyes. "Thanks for the cookies you sent to my apartment. I was thrilled to find those when I got home. It was dinner since I'm too damn tired to get anything else. I'll eat healthier tomorrow."

"You're welcome and eating cookies for dinner one night's not going to kill you."

Luke laughs and shows me the empty box.

"I think it's great you want to work with kids," Kolton says. "Good luck with your program."

"Thanks, man," Luke says.

"You should go to bed," I tell him. "Get well rested to save some kids' lives."

"I will," he says with a yawn. Seeing my brother yawn makes me sleepy too, and I lean back against Kolton without thinking. Of course, ever-observant Luke notices. "So...are you two going out? How's that gonna affect the play auditions?"

"Yes," I say. "There are no rules against it, so we'll be fine."

"That's right," Kolton agrees. "And if there were, I'd quit the workshop to keep seeing Lydia if that's what it took."

I gently nudge Kolton with my elbow. "No, you're not quitting the workshop."

Luke nods. "Okay then. I've gotta go. Lydia, keep taking care of yourself, and Kolton, be good to her so I won't have to use my extensive medical knowledge for evil."

Kolton laughs while I assure my brother that not only do I have a handle on my life, but Kolton's been a perfect gentleman the whole time I've known him.

I end the call and turn to Kolton, who is grinning at me, and I smile back. "What?"

"I've never had anyone's brother subtly threaten to kill me before. It's sweet that he's so protective of you. Were you two close growing up?"

"So, someone's brother less subtly threatened to kill you?"

Kolton laughed and shook his head.

"We were fine as kids. Luke split his time between his mom and dad, so we had a break from living together every other week. We went to the same school, but he's five years older, so we didn't exactly run in the same crowds. He was awesome at helping me understand algebra and anything related to biology or chemistry. Plus, my friends thought he was cute."

"Well, I've never had to threaten anyone's life for my sister. She could probably take me in a fight, easy."

"I can't see you hitting a woman, even your sister when you were kids."

"Nah, never did. She pelted me with shoes and toys plenty of times, but I'll admit I was a pain in the ass always playing jokes and pestering her."

I try to stifle another yawn as I lean back on the couch with Kolton. "Sorry. It's been a long day, and I'm exhausted. Thanks for letting me crash your night with Kendra. I really needed a friend."

"Of course," he says, tightening his arms around me. "I'm here if you ever want to talk or not talk about what's going on."

Despite having said I didn't want to talk about my day, I find myself ready to open up even more to Kolton. So, I do. I tell him about my realization of how selfish I'd been when I was hurting and what it must have done to my mother. I rehash the therapy assignment and writing the letter to Jason to say goodbye for real and how much lighter I felt after having done that.

Our revelations go both ways because he tells me more about the fears he'd carried after Maisy cheated on him and his worries about not living up to the image of being the man he'd been raised to be.

It's the type of conversation so effortless that several hours can pass in what feels like only minutes. There are no awkward silences or that feeling like you're just waiting for the other person to shut up so you can leave.

When I blink my eyes open, I'm still on Kolton's couch, curled up with him. It's daylight, and my neck is stiff from sleeping at a weird angle. I hear the sound of my phone buzzing on the trunk. I struggle to reach over a sleeping Kolton to answer it, but I don't make it in time. He stirs and hands my phone to me, and I'm horrified to see five missed calls from my mother. It's after seven and she must be so worried about me.

"Oh shit!" I say as I pull myself up. "My mom's going to kill me."

"I'm sorry. I didn't mean to fall asleep."

"Me neither." I tap my mom's name on my phone's favorites list, and she answers right away.

"Lydia!" she says. "Thank God! I woke up and realized your car wasn't here, and there was no log of you in the alarm system. And then I tracked your phone, and you wouldn't answer."

"I'm so sorry, Mom. I fell asleep at Kolton's apartment, and my phone was on silent. We just woke up, so I'll head home now. I want to talk to you about something and apologize in person. Be there soon as I can, okay?"

"I'll be here," she says before ending the call.

"She sounded upset," Kolton says.

"Yeah. I moved back in with her and my stepfather after college and was planning to stay for the summer to save money while I decided about grad school. Then Marienne and...well, everything went to shit, and I made that really big mistake. After I got out of the hospital, I agreed to stay at home for at least a year. It's not like I have a curfew or anything, but I've always let her know when I was staying out all night before."

"You sleep on other people's couches often?" Kolton asks with one eyebrow raised.

I playfully shove him backward and he pulls me with him. "Hardly ever, and yours was the most uncomfortable."

He laughs and lets me up. "Well, next time you sleep over, the bed's a lot more comfortable."

I know I'm blushing, but at the same time, I also know I'll be staying over again soon. It just feels right. "Well, I have to go seek forgiveness from my mother for more things than just freaking her out this morning. I'd kiss you goodbye, but my breath is awful."

"I'm sure mine's gross too." Kolton laughs again as he pulls me into a hug at his door. "Drive safely and let me know if you want to come out to my parents' place for fireworks later. Nine o'clock."

"You know what? I'll be there. My parents usually go to my step-uncle's house, but I would much rather hang out with you. Can I bring anything?"

"Great. Just bring yourself."

"I'll see if I can find her first!" Kolton brushes my hair out of my face and kisses me on the forehead. I hate that the gesture reminds me of Jason, and I have to close my eyes to push the thought away. Kolton is not Jason; he won't hurt me, and he won't leave me like Jason did. Everything is still new, but I know in my heart we'll stay friends even if we don't end up staying together. I may have to remind myself every day until I believe it enough to stop being afraid.

Chapter 30
March 18, 2023

I was more at peace during the second semester of my senior year than any other. My classes were great, and my production rehearsals were going well. I was paired with Cameron, and we were the leads in *Romeo and Juliet*. Since it was a role I'd played before, I knew I could perfect my performance, even without the extra rehearsals. And as a stage kissing partner, Cameron wasn't too bad since we'd been friends and only friends since our freshman year.

Jason had started hanging around the apartment a lot too. He'd made peace with Marienne, and he'd been nothing but friendly with me. Of course, I'd caught him looking at me when he thought I wasn't paying attention, but I didn't acknowledge it. Marienne was dating a guy named Ben, so all four of us played board games a few times. It felt like double dates, except without the physical affection at the end.

I had to admit, I still loved Jason and wanted to be with him again. I was honest when he'd asked how I felt about him at the beginning of our reacquaintance, so everything was dependent on him. We hadn't been alone together since the evening in January. He only came over when Marienne was home and left if she did. But we texted a lot. Mostly funny memes and daily check-ins, but nothing like the deep conversations I craved from years ago. I still missed him despite seeing him more than I ever had.

When he showed up the Saturday evening before spring break to deliver my Bite Squad order, I was surprised to see him.

"I didn't know you were delivering tonight," I said as he stepped inside, holding two bags. "Wait, that's too much food."

"I'm trying to save up some money before the summer, so I thought it would be good to pick up a few shifts during break. I saw your order and got some food for me too. Thought we could hang out for a while tonight if you didn't have other plans."

"Marienne's not here," I said, hesitating before closing the door.

Jason chuckled and took the food to the coffee table. "I think we can survive without a chaperone. Come on, let's eat and find something to watch on Netflix. It's been a long week."

We talked about classes, the ones I was taking and the ones Jason was teaching while we mindlessly watched a documentary about social media. We were about an hour into viewing when Jason grabbed the remote and turned off the television. "I didn't figure you were watching either," he said into the darkened room.

"Not really." I hear him shuffle nearer and then feel his hands on my face.

"There you are," he said, caressing my cheeks with his thumbs. "It's darker than I expected."

I couldn't tell how dark it was because having him touch me again was almost too much to take, and I'd closed my eyes the second his skin connected with mine.

"What are you thinking about?" he asked, still holding my face.

"How much I miss you."

"But I'm right here."

"Are you? Really? It's been so long since you've touched me, and I want that more than anything. I want us to be together."

His lips brushed my forehead first and then he pulled me closer and kissed my lips. I halfway thought I was dreaming, but then his hands found my waist and I knew it was real. My heart was pounding as he picked me up and carried me to my bedroom.

Jason unwrapped me like a precious gift, taking care to touch every part of my body, and all I could do was let him. I cried the entire time I let him have me. I'd wanted to be possessed by him for so long, and that's how it felt—like he cared and wanted to make love to me, not just get laid. He loved me. I was convinced of it at that moment.

Afterward, I wanted him to stay the night with me, but he said he needed to pick up a few late-night deliveries, so he had to go. He kissed me before he left, and I went to sleep happier than I'd ever been.

Vicki came up beside me while I was stocking shelves the next day at the dollar store. She was dressed for spring despite the weather being cool and rainy. She plopped down on the floor beside me and rattled on about her spring break trip she'd be leaving on the next day with Denton and his family.

"I'm happy for you," I told her. "Florida sounds like a lot of fun. I hope it's a lot less rainy and much warmer down south."

"Oh, it will be," she said. "I wish you could come with me."

"I know, but I need to save my time off for the trip to Europe with Marienne after we graduate. I wish you could go with us."

"If it wasn't for the flying part, I would. Taking a twelve-hour road trip is one thing, but I'm still terrified of going on a plane. You two will have to FaceTime with me when you see all the beautiful things."

"As long as you don't mind the time difference." I finished the shelf and started picking up the plastic packaging.

Vicki studied me closely and then broke into a grin.

"What is it?" I asked, looking down at my smock. "Do I have crazy hair, or something stuck to my face?"

"No. You just look so happy. Like you're glowing or something. I know that look on you since I've seen it before. You've got the 'in love' look. Did you meet someone?"

I'm not sure what my face looked like before, but I knew it was blushing. "I didn't realize you could see it in my face, but nothing's changed with who I love, Vic."

Her smile faded. "Oh, Lydia," she said. "Did something happen with him?"

I didn't like the feeling of being chastised, and I didn't want to talk about it in the middle of the store, so I asked Vicki to go outside to her truck. I met her there after I told the manager I was taking my break.

"It's not like last time," I told Vicki as we sat in her truck to stay out of the drizzle. "We've been seeing a lot of each other and texting all the time. Nothing happened at all until last night, and it was so sweet, Vic. I think he's sorry for what happened before. I can just tell he loves me despite how scared he was of commitment. I think he's truly ready for a relationship with me now."

"Did he say that?"

I didn't want to answer, but I had to. "Actions speak louder than words."

"His actions and words haven't always been aligned. You were so sad, and you were finally starting to seem happy again."

"Maybe I'm happy again because the man I love has finally come back into my life. Isn't that what you said when I first started seeing him? That if it was meant to be then he'd finally come around?"

"I'm not trying to hurt your feelings. I just don't want you to get hurt again, and he really didn't treat you right before. It would take a lot for him to convince me he's changed."

"Well, he doesn't have to convince you," I told her, opening the truck door. "I love him, Vicki, and I think he deserves another chance. I've gotta get back to work. Have fun on vacation, and I'll see you when you get back."

She started to say something, but I'd already shut the door to head back inside. It wasn't up to her or anyone else what I did with my heart or my body. Jason and I were together again, and it was all that mattered to me.

Chapter 31
July 4, 2024

Mom's sitting on the loveseat in our living room when I get home. She's holding a large mug of coffee and her hands shake as she places it on the end table. I feel terrible for all the pain I've caused her, not just now or last year, or all through college, but my whole life. I want to take it all back, but I know I can't. I walk over and take a seat beside her.

"I'm sorry, Mom. I don't even know where to start with all the apologies I owe you."

"It's okay. I overreacted. You're an adult, and I can't keep tracking you like you're still in high school. I have to accept you're grown up."

"But part of growing up is acknowledging how incredibly selfish I've been and how I've caused you so much fear and pain with everything. I'm so, so sorry I tried to kill myself last year. I wasn't thinking about anyone but myself and trying to end my pain. It never occurred to me what it would have done to you. I hope you can forgive me."

My mom's cheeks seem to melt into a waterfall of tears before she covers her face with her hands and starts sobbing. All I can do is wrap my arms around her and wait for her to stop.

"Oh, Lyddie," she whispers into my ear. "I love you so much."

"I love you too, Mom."

"I know you weren't thinking clearly back then. Leaving you at the psychiatric hospital after you'd recovered from the overdose was one of the hardest things I've ever done. Even though I had power of attorney for medical, I still couldn't visit you with you being an adult. It was heartbreaking listening to you cry on the phone, knowing I couldn't help you."

"You did help me, though, by sending me there so I could start getting better. I don't think I was thinking clearly for a while before the overdose. Letting Jason back into my life after he'd hurt me so much was stupid. I should have left him in my past and worked with a therapist a long time ago to get through everything I was feeling."

"You were in love, baby, and no one can fault you for that," Mom said. "I knew he wasn't good for you, but there was no way you'd listen to me. It was a lesson you had to learn for yourself. I'd have done anything to take away your pain though. I shouldn't have left you alone so soon after the accident. I knew you were devastated. I'm so sorry. I should have realized how close you were to spiraling out of control."

"It's not your fault, Mom. I felt like I'd lost everything even though I was still surrounded by people who loved me. Marienne and Jason were such big parts of my life I didn't think I could go on without them. I know now that's not true, but it was all I could see and feel last year."

"I know how hard it is to lose people you love, Lydia. Having you to care for was what got me through losing your father so suddenly."

"I'm sorry I wasn't as strong as you, but I'm stronger now. I don't ever want to give you a reason to be ashamed of me or give Dad a reason if he's watching over me. I promise I'll never be so careless with my life again."

"I know you won't. And, sweetheart, I think your dad watching over you helped save your life. You seem to be in a better place than you have since high school with the antidepressants and the different birth control. It didn't even occur to me until the doctor mentioned it in the hospital that your pills could be making your depression symptoms worse."

"I thought I was just sad because the guy I loved didn't love me back. I still can't shake the connection I felt to him though.

Everything logical tells me I shouldn't still love him, but I do, and I'm still working through it with Dr. Benson. I think I'm finally ready to move on and give love another chance."

It feels good to talk to Mom again, so I tell her everything about the summer so far. The visits to the cemetery, writing the letter to Jason and reading it to him, how I feel about Kolton. She nods and listens, but I can see the fear in her eyes when I mention talking to Jason. I worry she thinks I'm really not strong enough to move on.

"What is it, Mom?" I ask. "You look worried."

She picks up her mug even though I know it's empty. She just wants something to hold to buy herself more time to think before responding. "Have you told Dr. Benson about speaking to Jason at the cemetery?"

"We've talked about it."

"And what did she have to say?"

"She thinks it's good I'm working through feelings about the time I spent with him. I know it's not healthy to keep living in the past or expecting any future relationship to be like that."

Mom sighs and then smiles as she nods her head. "Is that where Kolton comes in? Are you planning to start a relationship with him?"

I can't hide my grin. "I haven't been attracted to anyone this way since Jason. It's still new, and we started out as friends, so everything just feels right. I'm going to meet his mom tonight, and I've already met his dad and his twin sister."

"Are you sleeping with him?"

"Mom!"

"I just don't want to see you rush into anything and get hurt again."

"Mom, I haven't been with anyone but Jason, so it's been more than a year since I've had sex. It's like I'm starting all over again, but I promise you I'm not going to rush into anything. I'll be much more careful with my body and my heart from now on."

She pulls me into her arms again and squeezes me tightly. "Well, you should bring Kolton over soon so Larry and I can meet him. Too bad Luke's so far away."

"Well, Luke actually met him via FaceTime last night and threatened physical harm if Kolton wasn't good to me."

Mom releases me except for her hands on my shoulders. "I want you to be happy more than anything, Lydia."

"I'm happier than I've been for as long as I can remember. The workshop is great, and the director thinks Kolton and I will get the lead roles. And even if we don't, we might get secondary roles."

Mom's eyes light up. "I'm thrilled for you, and I'm also going to miss you so much while you're on tour."

"I'll check in as often as I can, and I won't leave until September. And one of the stops is in Nashville, so you and Larry could probably see Luke in Memphis and just make a trip of it."

She hugs me again. "We'll have to do that."

Later, a knock on my door wakes me from a mid-afternoon nap. I'm disoriented as I grab my phone to check the time, disturbing Roscoe in the process. He huffs at me and snuggles down into my pillow. Phoebe pokes her head in and is surprised to find me in bed, still fully clothed from the day before. I haven't spoken to her since our lunch together when she'd told me about her engagement.

"Oh, no!" she says. "Your mom let me in, but she didn't tell me you were sick."

"It's fine. I'm not sick. I was just up late and woke up super early, so I didn't get a lot of sleep. I still need to shower."

"Oh, good!" She plops down on my bed, jostling me and Roscoe, who sighs at her. She rewards him with a scratch behind the ears. "You should come out to the lake with Sam and me tonight. His brother's going to be there with some of his friends. It'll be fun. I wanted to save you from the yearly event with your awful stepcousins."

"No, thanks. I'm meeting Kolton's mom tonight. I've already met his dad and sister."

"Sounds serious..."

I fill her in on everything that's happened with Kolton since I last spoke to her, but I keep his virginity to myself. I like having a secret between us, and it's really no one else's business.

"I'm a little nervous about meeting his mom since I know it's coming. The other meetings were by chance."

Phoebe laughs. "It's likely she already knows about Kolton's dad walking in on y'all making out."

"Don't remind me. I'm not usually one for full-on PDA."

"Well, a darkened workshop isn't exactly a place for an exhibitionist anyway, and you two thought you were alone. Maybe it's good you were interrupted so it didn't get too hot and heavy too fast. Give it some time before you jump into bed with him. He'll wait if he's worth it."

If she only knew. "Well, I kinda slept over at his apartment last night. Completely unintentionally, and it freaked out my mom when she couldn't reach me. Nothing happened, we just fell asleep, but it was nice waking up in his arms. I've never got to have that before, and honestly, it was better than sex."

"Sounds like you haven't had really great sex yet."

"Eww. I can't think about you and Sam having sex. He's like a brother to me."

"I know, I know. But soon enough you'll be telling me about all the hot sex you're having with Kolton, and all will be forgotten."

"I'm scared, Phoebe." I drop my hands to Roscoe's belly and start rubbing him gently. He groans appreciatively. "I didn't think I'd find a relationship, and Kolton is so nice and normal. What if he can't handle my seven shades of crazy?"

"Don't say that."

"But I'm not okay yet. The medicine helps, and I've been in therapy for a while now. I've also been talking to Jason at the cemetery since the anniversary of the accident."

Phoebe takes my hands and squeezes them as Roscoe looks up to figure out why the belly rub has stopped. "Does your therapist know about you talking to Jason?"

I nod. "I told my mom too, and Kolton knows I'm still working on everything. Dr. Benson suggested I write a letter when we were talking about my father's death, but I actually ended up writing a letter to Jason. I read it to him at the cemetery, and I'm not planning to talk to him again. I probably won't go there anymore—at least not alone—and I hope Marienne would understand I don't have to go there to remember her. Like I said, I'm crazy."

Phoebe sighs and releases my hands to grab my shoulders. "Lydia, the fact you can admit you're trying proves you're not crazy. And you have every right to be scared. That's why I keep telling you to take things slowly with Kolton to avoid getting hurt again. Don't you remember what your grandma said years ago when we spent the night with her and were fantasizing about when we'd meet our future husbands?"

I smile at the memory of Grammy's sage advice. "Yes, I do. She said, 'Stop looking for your prince charming, and let him find you.'"

"Exactly. Sam asked me out, and I gave him a chance. Kolton asked you out, so you're giving him a chance, and it sounds like you have feelings for him. It's been over a year since the accident and your..." She looks at me like she's afraid to say the words.

"Suicide attempt," I finish for her. "It's okay to talk about it. I'm not in a bad place anymore, and honestly, I don't remember a lot about the couple of days before it. I can promise you I want to live, Phoebe. I was just hurting so much at the time I guess I couldn't see past it. I'm sorry for the pain I caused you by being selfish about my own. Can you forgive me?"

Now Phoebe's crying as she pulls me into her arms. "No apologies are needed, Lyds," she says through her tears. "You're my best friend; I love you."

"I love you too."

After Phoebe leaves, I call Vicki for a similar conversation that leaves us both crying. Later, I hop in the shower to wash away all the emotions of the morning. I know there'll be more because I have to talk to Kolton and tell him the truth about everything before I can move forward with him. I haven't lied to him exactly but lies by omission can feel just as bad. And maybe it's me I've been lying to by refusing to say something important out loud.

Chapter 32
May 12, 2023

Commencement was Saturday morning. And the Friday night before, I was lying in my bed in Jason's arms. He wasn't usually one to cuddle after making love, and I was reveling in the moment as he caressed my bare arm. I could tell he was deep in thought and would have given anything to know what was on his mind.

Marienne and I would leave for Europe on Monday, so I wanted to spend as much time with Jason as possible before being gone for almost two weeks.

"So, did you decide what you're gonna do this summer?" I asked.

"I'm sure I'll find something to keep busy," he said. "I'm not sure yet if I'll teach a class second summer term or not. They don't need me for the first term. I might just load up on Bite Squad orders for all the college kids staying for classes or the summer campers. Should be enough money to get me by."

"Marienne and I are supposed to move out of this place by the end of the month. I'm thinking about talking to the landlord to see if I can stay longer and pay the extra rent until a one-bedroom opens up."

"Why would you want to stay here? I thought you wanted to take a year off before grad school and live with your parents to save money on rent."

"That was the original plan back in January, but a lot of things have changed since then. I don't want to be so far away from you by transferring my job back to a store near my parents' house."

"It's not that far away, and I don't think you should be making plans based on what I'm doing. I don't even know what I'm doing."

"Jason, why wouldn't I consider my boyfriend in my plans? It's not exactly unusual."

He sat up to turn on the lamp and then looked at me with wide eyes. "Lydia, I'm not..."

My heart sank. "Sure, I get it, you don't like labels, but we're together now, aren't we Jason?"

"Together in the physical sense right at this moment, Lydia, but we haven't made any long-term commitments. I realized a while ago I didn't want to be tied down so young. We have a lot of chemistry, and this has been fun, but it might not last the way our friendship can."

I felt sick. "I don't understand...you knew...you know how I feel about you. I thought you were just scared before and..." I couldn't talk anymore. I couldn't think straight and couldn't feel anything except the pounding of my heart and the cold sweat that had broken out on my skin. I thought I might pass out or throw up at any second.

Had I misjudged what we had? I'd been sure we were together. He'd known the whole time how much I loved him. I told him all the time. And every time we made love, I'd told him without words. I had to have been sucked into a parallel universe where nothing made sense anymore because I'd waited so long for him to come around, and he finally had. Hadn't he? No. Something wasn't right.

After a minute or two, I realized Jason was talking to me. I didn't know what he was saying when I reached out and touched his lips with my finger. "Stop," I told him.

He sucked in a breath and closed his eyes, tucking his chin to his chest.

"I love you, Jason, and I want to spend the rest of my life with you. Do you love me? I need an answer."

When he looked at me, I felt like every bit of the pathetic, bawling child I was as I stared into his glassy eyes. But he didn't speak.

"Get out of here, you coward! I don't want to talk to you or see you again until you can finally tell me flat out you don't love me or admit you do and are just too fucking scared to have anything real!" I got out of bed and stumbled to the bathroom, not caring that I was still naked. I turned on the shower so he wouldn't hear me break down.

Somehow, I managed to shut off my thoughts and get through graduation without losing my mind in anger and heartbreak. I saw Jason from afar since Marienne was graduating too, but I didn't get close enough to say anything to him. Not that I would have. It was up to him. Because I was determined to be with him forever if he could say the three little words I longed to hear or learn to live without him if he couldn't.

Vicki was there to cheer us on since her ceremony would come in December after her student-teaching internship. My parents, my stepbrother, and Marienne's parents all came back to our apartment for a celebration of our hard work.

Marienne and Ben had broken up, so she and I made a pact to avoid the topic of our ill-fated lovers and just have an amazing time in Europe. And we did. It was the best time I could have imagined. I walked on streets, entered buildings, and admired artwork older than anything I'd ever seen before.

We laughed and enjoyed the most delicious food as we took in all the sights with our college tour group. Marienne and I were the only young women from Arkansas, and everyone else in our group made comments about our cute accents. We were thrilled to be able to see places we'd only dreamt of before.

The only time I let myself cry during the whole trip was when I made a wish at the Trevi Fountain in Italy. I wished for happiness and love in my future even if it didn't include Jason.

Marienne didn't scold me but instead bought me gelato before we continued sightseeing. Being surrounded by buildings and places centuries old made me feel so much smaller in the world, and it was exactly the trip I needed.

After returning from Europe, Marienne and I packed the remainder of the things our parents hadn't taken home with them after graduation. We headed to our parents' houses to prepare to sort out the rest of our lives. When Marienne called the day before my birthday and said she needed to see me to tell me something important, I waited until long after she said she'd arrive.

Several hours passed and I still couldn't reach her. I tried texting Jason, but he didn't respond either. And Marienne's parents only knew she'd planned to drive to my house. They promised to get in touch when they heard from her. I stayed awake all night and didn't hear anything until early the next morning. By then, I already knew something was wrong but hadn't imagined how bad it actually was.

I want to be with Kolton, but I need to tell him everything first. The only thing that makes sense is to take him to the cemetery with me for my last visit. I don't want to do it alone.

Thankfully, Kolton agrees to let me pick him up on the way to Russellville. He's smiling as I watch him walk down the outside staircase and head toward my car. After he gets in, he leans over to kiss me.

"I've had time to brush now," he says. "Hope my breath is better than it was this morning."

"Much better. Thanks for coming with me."

"Of course."

I leave the parking lot and make my way to the interstate. Once I'm out of heavy traffic and able to set cruise control, Kolton reaches over and takes my hand, and we stay that way for the rest of the drive without talking anymore.

When I park at the cemetery, there's no one else there I can see, and I'm glad Kolton and I will be alone. I take him to the bench beside Marienne's grave. The flowers I left for the past several weeks are lined up in gradient colors as they've faded in the sun. Kolton looks down at the stone and reads it aloud.

"Marienne Elaine Caldwell, beloved daughter." He puts his arm around my waist and pulls me close. "Only twenty-one years old and about a month shy of her birthday. It's tragic. I'm sorry you lost your friend."

"I thought it was my fault because she was driving to my parents' house that night to see me when the accident happened. It was the night before my birthday."

"That doesn't make it your fault, Lydia. That's why it's called an accident."

"I know now, but at the time I was so devastated from losing her and Jason, I couldn't forgive myself, and then...well, you know what happened next."

"Wait, so is that why things ended with Jason? He blamed you for the accident. That's really messed up."

I feel a slight stinging in my eyes as I take Kolton's hand, but I don't feel like crying. "No. That's not it. I've been trying to forgive myself for the pain I caused my family and other friends. I had ended things with Jason a couple of weeks before the accident when he couldn't tell me the truth about how he felt about me. I called him a coward that night and said he shouldn't talk to me again unless he could tell me the truth."

"Has he told you now?"

"I'll never know because he can't tell me, and that's part of why it's been so hard to move on."

Kolton furrows his brow. "He's never told you if he loves you, after all this time?"

I shake my head and take Kolton's hand. I pull him past Marienne's grave to the row of plots behind hers. I haven't been to this side of the cemetery since the day of the funeral more than a year ago. I kneel beside a headstone with an intricate dream catcher engraved on top and look up at Kolton.

Once Kolton reads the inscription, his jaw tightens and he squats beside me, placing his hand on my shoulder. "Oh, my God," he whispers. "Lydia..."

I trace the engraved letters and numbers on the stone.

Jason Allan Caldwell
February 2, 1997 — May 29, 2023

I've blocked out most of my last birthday since it was the day I learned about the accident. It was gut-wrenching losing one of my best friends and the man I loved at the same time. The memories come floating back, but I feel at peace now. Finally.

Marienne's parents were there with Jason's parents at the joint funeral. I'd also met Jason's older brother, his sister-in-law, and his nieces for the first time that day. I can't remember their names now. My parents were with me, and Phoebe. Luke too, but when I think about it, I can't recall a word anyone said to me during the graveside service. Vicki wasn't able to be there, but I'd spoken with her on the phone during the drive to the cemetery.

The whole day had felt like swimming through a fog with everyone's voices both loud and muffled at the same time. I know I spoke to people in the family and expressed condolences and recognized that my pain probably wasn't the worst among the people there. Seeing parents bury their children isn't the natural order of things. We were all somber and broken, drowning in the unique grief only possible after losing two people far too young to die.

I stand and walk back to the bench on Marienne's side. Kolton follows and sits beside me, taking my hand.

"I know you probably think I'm crazy and have a ton of questions."

"I don't think you're crazy, but I don't understand why you didn't tell me he was gone."

"Jason's dead. He died the same night as Marienne when she was driving him to see me. I haven't been able to say it out loud to anyone until now, despite my therapist pushing me to say it to her. And it's not that I don't know the truth. I just wasn't ready to admit it. I don't know why he'd tagged along or what he planned to say, but the truth is, we were never together the way I wanted us to be."

I tell Kolton everything about coming to the cemetery for the first time since the funeral earlier this summer and imagining what it would be like to see Jason again. Speaking to Jason as if he were still alive had helped me to come to terms with a lot of my emotions about our relationship. I needed more time to analyze what had happened between us and talking it over and writing the letter to him finally helped me let him go.

Kolton listens without interruption, and he doesn't act like he wants to run away, which is more than I can expect. When I finish rehashing, I wipe the tears from my face and take a deep, cleansing breath.

"I don't even know what else to say except I'm so sorry," he says quietly and exhales with a slight whistle.

"Kolton, with everything I've told you, I understand if you don't want to date me anymore. I've gotta be one of the most fucked-up people you've ever met."

I don't expect laughter, but as Kolton chuckles and embraces me, I feel the last bit of anxiety fade away. "Lydia, we're all fucked-up in one way or another, and I'm glad we found each other."

"I'll be okay," I tell him. "I promise I'll keep up with therapy and take meds as long as I need to. I've had more pain than I'd like at twenty-three, but I hope it's made me stronger or at least strong enough to stop running away from joy."

"I'm happy to hear that. I know we've only known each other for a month, but I've never felt like this before, Lydia. It's like we've always known each other, and even if you decide later that we should only be friends, I want you in my life always, okay?"

"I want that too."

"Then I think we're gonna be okay." He kisses my forehead and then we head back to my car.

Epilogue
August 14, 2024

Kolton went as my date to Vicki's wedding last month and we had the best time dancing late into the evening. She was a gorgeous bride. I got choked up giving her wedding toast talking about our late friend Marienne, who'd said several years ago Vicki deserved a life full of unicorns and rainbows. I wanted it for her.

Dr. Benson is pleased with my progress and feels comfortable continuing our sessions over the phone if I need her in the future. I was finally able to speak to her about Jason's death, and she was right that everything's been a little easier since then. Really, things got easier after I spoke with Kolton on Independence Day.

I'll start a year of living my life out of suitcases with Kolton the day after Labor Day, and I couldn't be more excited. The workshop is over, and we earned the lead roles in the new play, *When Does Life Begin?* We're still not allowed to speak about it even after getting advanced copies of our parts in the first act. Rehearsals in Chicago will take up the rest of the year, and we'll start touring in early 2025.

Nel and Tom will be on the tour with us, having scored secondary parts. Jake and Tanya weren't selected for this play, but Bernetta knew some casting agents for other productions and sent some recommendations for them. We've got a running group text full of acting memes to keep in touch that I hope will last.

I'll get to toast Phoebe and Sam at their wedding this weekend. The best thing I can wish for them is a lifetime of happiness, love, and friendship. Because what else can you wish for friends you've loved forever?

That's how I feel about Kolton—like I've known him and loved him forever. He's easy to love and isn't shy about showing affection or introducing me as his girlfriend. When Kolton told me he loved me right before our final auditions, I was ready to say it too. We didn't feel the need to be cautious with our hearts anymore—at least not with each other.

We fit and share the same dreams for a future together, and I couldn't imagine a better partner. I'll never forget the day we heard about our successful auditions. After sharing our joy with family and friends, we spent the rest of the evening celebrating each other. The connection when we made love for the first time was what I'd been waiting for my whole life.

All my fears about finding someone to share my life with were unfounded. I thought if Jason didn't love me, then no one ever would. But really, having outside love in my life was never the problem. There were people who loved me then, those who love me now, and those who will in the future.

I don't know if Kolton's love for me will last a lifetime like I'm sure mine will for him, but I do know I'll be okay. My main problem was always not loving myself enough.

ABOUT THE AUTHOR:

Brandi Easterling Collins grew up in Arkansas where she still resides with her husband, two children, and their two dogs. When she's not writing or reading, she enjoys spending time with her family, thrift store shopping, painting, drawing, and leisurely walks outside.

When Does Life Begin? is her fifth novel. Her other novels include *Caroline's Lighthouse*, *Jordan's Sister*, *What I Learned That Summer*, and *One Shot*.

For more information about future publications, visit caniscareyou.com.